It was impossible to ignore him completely

"Are you going to Huancayo?" Sara asked him. She might feel less nervous if she found out something about him.

He grinned. "I wasn't until half an hour ago—when I spotted you standing there at the station."

"But—you can't have got on this train just because of me!" she spluttered. "It—it doesn't make any sense."

"It makes perfect sense to me," he said in an affable voice.

"You don't even know me!"

"Of course not. But we've got ten hours to get over that small hurdle." Lucas's mouth relaxed into a strange smile. "You see, I think you're the woman I've been waiting for, Sara Lambert."

JOANNA MANSELL finds writing hard work but very addictive. When she's not bashing away at her typewriter, she's usually got her nose buried in a book. She also loves gardening and daydreaming, two pastimes that go together remarkably well. The ambition of this Essex-born author is to write books that people will enjoy reading.

Books by Joanna Mansell

HARLEQUIN PRESENTS
1116—MIRACLE MAN
1139—LORD AND MASTER
1156—ILLUSION OF PARADISE
1186—THE THIRD KISS
1218—WILD JUSTICE
1250—NIGHT WITH A STRANGER

HARLEQUIN ROMANCE
2836—THE NIGHT IS DARK
2866—SLEEPING TIGER
2894—BLACK DIAMOND

Don't miss any of our special offers. Write to us at the following address for information on our newest releases.

Harlequin Reader Service
901 Fuhrmann Blvd., P.O. Box 1397, Buffalo, NY 14240
Canadian address: P.O. Box 603,
Fort Erie, Ont. L2A 5X3

JOANNA MANSELL

the seduction of sara

Harlequin Books

TORONTO • NEW YORK • LONDON
AMSTERDAM • PARIS • SYDNEY • HAMBURG
STOCKHOLM • ATHENS • TOKYO • MILAN

Harlequin Presents first edition August 1990
ISBN 0-373-11291-2

Original hardcover edition published in 1989
by Mills & Boon Limited

CHAPTER ONE

SARA looked a little anxiously at her fiancé. 'You do understand why I have to go to South America, don't you, Edward?'

'Of course I understand,' he said, with a small frown. 'But I must say that it was very inconsiderate of your father to leave his affairs in this sort of mess.'

'Yes, it was inconsiderate,' Sara agreed flatly. 'He never could think straight, though, where my stepmother was concerned.'

Then she gave a silent sigh. How could she possibly explain to Edward her father's obsession with her stepmother? She didn't even understand it herself. She only knew that her father had never had any love to spare for her, his only child. His feelings had been completely wrapped up with the woman who had walked out on him over twenty years ago.

Now, her father had died, very suddenly and unexpectedly, and on top of the shock of his death had come another bombshell. He had never changed his will. Everything that Sara had always assumed would be hers—the house in which she had lived all her life, the small pieces of jewellery that had a deeply sentimental value, the personal items that no one else could possibly treasure the way she would—had all been left to her stepmother, whom Sara couldn't remember, but whom she hated with an intensity that was quite foreign to her nature.

Sara's own mother had died when she was born. A year later, her father had remarried, but it hadn't lasted. Just eighteen months later, his new wife had walked out on him. Sara had no clear memories of her stepmother, and she had certainly never expected to have any contact with her again, not after all these years. Only now, she didn't have much choice. This woman, who was a complete stranger to her, owned everything that Sara held dear.

It wasn't fair! she told herself furiously, for the hundredth time since the solicitor had revealed the astonishing details of her father's will. And she was most certainly going to contest it!

Seeing the set look on her face, Edward took hold of her hand solicitously. Sara somehow managed to subdue her black mood, and smiled up at him. Dear Edward! He had been such a help during the very difficult and trying few weeks that she had just gone through.

Instead of pulling her closer and comforting her, though, Edward instead touched the ring which she wore on the third finger of her left hand. He had given it to her just a month ago, and if Sara had secretly thought the three diamonds in a plain setting just a little old-fashioned, she would never have dreamt of saying that to Edward. Of course he had chosen a very traditional type of ring. He was that sort of man. In fact, it was why Sara had been so attracted to him in the first place. His steadiness, his set views, his unemotional way of looking at things, all made her feel very safe. In fact, he was precisely the sort of man she wanted to marry. She had seen how out-of-control emotions could wreck someone's life, and she didn't intend to let that ever happen to her. She and Edward would suit each other extremely well.

'Perhaps it would be a good idea to leave your ring in my safe while you're away,' Edward suggested. 'You know what these South American countries are like—thieves on every corner. It is a rather expensive ring, and I know how upset you would be if you lost it.'

Sara blinked at him. 'Take off my ring?' she repeated a little blankly. 'But I love wearing it.'

'Of course you do, darling,' he said soothingly. 'That's why it makes good sense to take care of it.'

With some reluctance, Sara slowly slid the ring off her finger. She supposed Edward was right. He nearly always was. And she *would* hate to lose it. Seeing it sparkling on her finger made her feel cared for and secure.

Edward carefully placed it in the small wall safe. Then he turned back to her.

'What time is your flight?'

'Fairly early in the morning.'

'I'm sorry I can't come to the airport with you, but I've a very important meeting tomorrow. I really can't afford to miss it.'

'I'll be fine,' she said, forcing herself to sound resolute. 'And with luck, I won't be away for more than a couple of days. My solicitor's managed to trace my stepmother to a hotel in Lima. I should be able to fly there, get things sorted out, and then fly straight back home again.'

Edward's brows drew together. 'You're sure it wouldn't be better to wait until your stepmother returns to England?'

'I don't know how long that'll be, and I want to get this settled straight away. She might be in South America for weeks, and I can't wait that long. I hate being this uncertain about the future. I'm living in a house that doesn't belong to me any more, sleeping in a bed that isn't even mine——' For a moment, her voice nearly cracked, and Sara fought hard to control it. Edward hated outbursts of emotion. So did she, normally—but suddenly things weren't normal any more. Her life had been completely turned upside-down, and she knew she wouldn't have any peace of mind until she got it back to its usual steady level.

'What's your stepmother doing in South America?' asked Edward, giving a deeper frown. 'Just travelling around, seeing the sights? Strange place for a holiday,' he commented.

'She isn't on holiday,' replied Sara. 'She runs her own knitwear company. She's gone there to try and find ideas for a new range of ethnic designs. That's why her secretary didn't know when she would be back. Apparently she takes off now and then, travelling to different parts of the world, in search of inspiration. Sometimes she's gone for weeks, sometimes even for months.'

'It seems like a very funny way to run a business,' Edward remarked disapprovingly. 'I shouldn't think it's very successful. I doubt if you'll get back your inheritance without a fight, Sara. She's probably desperately short of money. She'll try and sell off the house, the contents, everything, to try and raise enough cash to keep her business floundering along for a while longer.'

'Then I'll stop her,' Sara declared, her eyes flashing with sudden brightness. 'That house, and everything in it, is *mine*. I love it. I won't give it up!'

Edward looked faintly surprised at her outburst, and Sara coloured slightly. She didn't usually let her feelings run away with her like that.

'If you can't break the will, at least you won't be thrown out on the streets,' he reassured her. 'We'll bring forward the date of our wedding. You'll have a new home, with me.'

'Thank you, Edward,' Sara said gratefully. 'You don't know what it means to me, having someone to care about me the way that you do.'

Edward instantly looked embarrassed, as he always did when she spoke of anything too personal.

'You know I'm very fond of you,' he said rather gruffly. Then he looked at his watch. 'I suppose you'd better go if you've got to catch an early flight tomorrow. You'll want to get a good night's sleep.'

He walked with her to the door. Then he gave her a light kiss on the cheek. 'Don't stay away too long,' he said, a little awkwardly. 'I'll miss you.'

Sara smiled up at him. 'I'll be back as soon as I can,' she promised.

As she got into her car, though, she gave a small shiver. Quite suddenly, she felt very much on her own. She looked at her bare finger, where Edward's ring should have been, and shivered again. Then she found herself wishing he *had* been able to come with her to the airport in the morning. Surely he could have postponed that meeting? argued a little voice inside her head.

Sara quickly told herself not to be so silly, and briskly started up the engine. Edward was a very busy man. She couldn't expect him to drop everything, just so he could see her on to a plane.

As she drove off, though, she suddenly shivered again. In the morning, she would be setting off to a strange country in search of a woman she didn't know, but who had affected her life in a hundred small and subtle ways. And when she found her she was going to have to fight her for her inheritance.

Sara wished that the next few days were already over, and she was safely back with Edward again.

* * *

The flight to South America was a long one, and left Sara with far too much time to brood over the upsetting events of the past few weeks. And she knew that she was still suffering from the shock of her father's sudden death, which had hit her in ways which she hadn't even expected. Although she had never been able to get close to him, at least she had known he was there if she needed him. Now, she was completely on her own.

No, not on your own, she argued fiercely with herself. You've got Edward. He's completely dependable; he'll never let you down. And yet, somehow, even that thought didn't lift her out of her depression.

Her mind wandered back to the house where she had been born and raised. Other people might not have thought it anything special, but she adored it. The rooms were low-ceilinged and cosy, the windows opened out on to a tangled garden of sweet-smelling flowers and old-fashioned roses, and the furniture was worn but comfortable. Sara had always cherished hopes that she and Edward would be able to live there after they were married, although she was well aware that it would be very difficult to prise Edward out of his exquisitely furnished and centrally heated flat.

But now it turned out that the house wasn't even hers, even though she had lived there for the whole of her twenty-four years. It had *never* been hers, because her father had always meant it to go to her stepmother. Sara was his only child, and yet he hadn't made any provision for her, hadn't given a thought as to what would happen to her after he had gone. All he had been able to think about was Clarissa— Sara's mouth set into a hard line as she said her stepmother's name out loud. He had spent just a year and a half with that woman, and yet she had haunted him for the rest of his life. He had never forgotten her; had probably never stopped hoping that she would come back. He had left everything he owned to her, as if he couldn't bear to break his ties with her even after he was dead. Sara found that kind of obsession quite terrifying. She was going to make very sure that nothing like that ever happened to *her*.

And now, she was finally going to come face to face with the woman who had caused her father so much grief and ruined his life. What would she be like? Still some sort of *femme fatale*, or would she be overblown and blowsy by this time? Sara hoped it was the latter. People who caused that sort of devastation deserved to have everything taken away from them.

By the time the plane landed at Lima she was tired and had a headache. After going through all the formalities she managed to get a taxi, and gave the driver the address of the hotel where Clarissa was staying.

Not long now, she told herself, and suddenly felt horribly nervous. She hated scenes, and she was afraid there was going to be a hell of a big one once Clarissa found out why she was here.

The taxi rattled its way through an urban sprawl, and Sara peered out of the window without much interest. Her headache was steadily getting worse, not helped by the weather, which was very humid.

When they finally reached the hotel, she had to force herself to go inside. She walked very slowly towards the reception desk, dumped her case on the floor, and then looked at the clerk.

'Do you speak English?' she asked.

'Yes, certainly,' he replied immediately, and Sara gave a weary sigh of relief.

'My name is Sara Lambert. I telephoned from London to reserve a room.'

The clerk confirmed her booking, whipped through the formalities, and produced the key to her room in just a couple of minutes. Sara took it, and wished she could just crawl up to her room and sleep for several hours. First, though, she had to get a couple of things sorted out.

'I believe there's someone staying here that I know,' she said in a stiff voice. 'Her name is—Clarissa Lambert.'

It was a real effort to get out the words. Sara had no idea why her stepmother still used her married name. Most women who were separated from their husbands reverted to their maiden name—especially when they had been separated for over twenty years!

The clerk's face instantly brightened, 'Ah, yes— Mrs Lambert. She did stay here for a couple of days. She left at the end of last week, though.'

'Left?' echoed Sara, with a touch of despair. 'But I've come all this way to see her——' Her voice broke off rather jerkily in mid-sentence, and she had to make an enormous effort to pull herself together. 'Do you know where she's gone?' she asked at last.

'Yes, I do. She has gone to Huancayo. Mrs Lambert was very interested in local crafts, and they have a large market there on Sundays.'

'Will she be coming back here, to this hotel?'

'I don't think so,' replied the clerk regretfully. It was clear that Clarissa had made quite an impression on him, and that he had been sorry to see her leave.

Sara's shoulders drooped tiredly. 'Then I suppose I'll have to follow her to Huancayo. Is it far? How do I get there?'

The clerk gave a shrug. 'There are buses—but I think perhaps a lady like you would prefer the train. It leaves early, though. Yóu should be at the station before seven o'clock if you want to be sure of getting a seat.'

Sara briefly closed her eyes. That was just what she *didn't* need—an early-morning start after that long flight. There didn't seem much alternative, though. Damn Clarissa! she thought with uncharacteristic venom. She certainly wasn't in the mood for chasing the wretched woman all over Peru.

'Do you know which hotel she'll be staying in, at Huancayo?'

'Certainly,' said the clerk promptly. 'I recommended it to her personally. I will write down the address for you. It is very clean, and very efficient— and run by my cousin,' he added helpfully. 'If you also wish to stay there, he will look after you.'

Sara picked up the sheet of paper with the address on it, and the key to her room, then she began to trudge wearily towards the stairs.

'I hope you find your friend,' the clerk called after her.

Sara gritted her teeth. Clarissa Lambert was no friend of hers—and never could be!

She slept badly, despite her tiredness, and had no trouble in getting up in time to catch the train. A taxi took her to the station, which already seemed to be full of people. Sara gripped her case and bag more tightly. The guide-book had warned her that thieves often operated at rail and bus stations. To have her money and papers stolen really would be the last straw.

The guide-book had also told her that the train journey to Huancayo took ten hours—and that was on a good day, when nothing went wrong! Having come this far, though, she wasn't going to go back home until she had made every possible effort to find Clarissa Lambert.

She took a fairly incurious look at the rest of the people crowding into the station. They were a mixture of Peruvians, most of them carrying large packages wrapped up in blankets, and tourists of all ages and nationalities, the majority of them toting backpacks, bed-rolls and other equipment, obviously seeing the country "on the cheap." She knew that Peru was popular with tourists, especially young people who were looking for something different. So far, though, Sara had remained impervious to the country's charms. She just wanted to find Clarissa Lambert, get things sorted out, and then head straight back home, to Edward.

The queue for the train was surprisingly orderly. As Sara took her place in it, she rather nervously eyed the people around her. She wasn't used to travelling on her own like this, especially in a strange country, and her nerves were beginning to feel very jumpy. Most of her fellow-travellers took very little notice of her, though. The backpackers mostly seemed to be in small groups, chatting away to each other, while the local Peruvians quietly and patiently waited for the train.

Then Sara's gaze alighted on a man who, like her, seemed to be completely on his own. She supposed he had caught her attention because he appeared to be particularly interested in *her*. His gaze was fixed on her quite unswervingly, and even when she glared straight back at him he didn't seem inclined to look away.

He was toting a large rucksack, and looked thoroughly disreputable. His denim jeans were clean, but torn and faded, and his old leather jacket wasn't in a much better state. A battered hat covered his hair, so that she couldn't see its colour, and his skin was burnt dark brown, as if he had spent most of the last few weeks in the open air.

Sara shot another disapproving look at him. She supposed he had been hiking his way around the country, sleeping rough most of the time. Heaven knew what he was doing here, queueing for the train. He looked as if he would have a lot of trouble scraping up enough money for the fare.

Since he still refused to look away from her, she quite deliberately turned her back on him. She certainly didn't want him coming up and trying to scrounge some money from her. That would be really embarrassing!

Then another—and more alarming—thought occurred to her. What if he had picked her out as easy game because she was obviously on her own? He could snatch her bag and be off with it before she could do anything about it.

She shuffled around nervously, and tried to edge closer to the group of backpackers nearest to her. With luck, he would think she was with them, and look for another, easier victim.

When she shot a nervous glance over her shoulder, though, she found he was still there, watching her. Worse than that, he had moved closer! He was only four or five yards away now, and her heart started to thump.

He wasn't a big man but he was tall, and she had the unnerving impression of a lean, powerful body hidden under that disreputable clothing. What nationality was he? she wondered. It was difficult to tell, with that dark, weathered skin and his face half hidden under that dreadful hat.

Sara swallowed hard, and wished the queue would move faster. There only seemed to be one man doling out the tickets, and she was still some distance away from him. She would feel a lot safer when she was actually on the train.

The queue shuffled forward a couple more paces, and Sara went to pick up her suitcase, not wanting to lose her place. Before she could touch it, though, a tanned hand curled round the handle and lifted it with ease.

'Let me carry it for you,' offered a deep male voice. 'It looks rather heavy.'

Sara lifted her head and found herself staring straight at the man who had been studying her with such interest. Her nerves quivered, and she made an effort to snatch the case away from him.

'I can manage perfectly well on my own,' she snapped. 'Go and help someone else, if you want to be a Good Samaritan.'

His eyes—which she could now see were a deep blue—rested on her calmly. 'I'd rather help you.'

Sara was still struggling to wrench the case away from him. Really, this was getting to be completely embarrassing! People were turning to look at them, and she hated being the centre of attention. With one final effort, she managed to haul her suitcase out of his grasp; then she took a couple of hurried steps back from him.

'I'm perfectly capable of carrying my own suitcase,' she informed him frostily. 'If you want to earn some money carrying people's luggage, go and try someone else!'

The man's dark blue eyes lost a little of their affa-bility. 'I don't recall asking you for any kind of payment.'

'No, you didn't,' she retorted. 'But I'm sure you wouldn't have turned down a large tip.'

He seemed about to say something equally sharp. At the last moment, though, he checked himself, and a slow smile spread over the flexible line of his mouth.

'If you're determined to be independent, there's not much I can do about it. But if any time you find you can't manage, remember that I'm around.'

He turned round and strolled off, and Sara watched him with definite unease. What had he meant by that? That he was going to hang about until the train actually left? Really, men like that shouldn't be allowed in a railway station! she told herself with some vehemence. There should be some sort of by-law that stopped them from wandering around and annoying legitimate passengers.

To her relief, the queue began to move forward a little faster. A few minutes later, she was clutching her first-class ticket and hurrying towards the train. If the journey was going to take ten hours, then she wanted to get a good seat.

The first-class carriage was hardly luxurious, but it had shiny padded seats set around tables, and plenty of luggage racks. That was probably just as well, reflected Sara, considering the amount of luggage that most people seemed to be carrying!

The racks were already bulging with backpacks and canvas holdalls, but there was a small space that looked as if it would just about take her suitcase. She was about to ask one of the backpackers if they would mind lifting her suitcase up for her, when a pair of strong hands lifted it from the floor and efficiently wedged it into the rack.

'Thank you,' began Sara. Then she turned round and found herself looking into a pair of deep blue eyes that were already disturbingly familiar.

'You!' she spluttered. 'How did you get on to the train?'

'Like you, I bought a ticket,' he replied in an unruffled voice. 'Is this your seat, by the window?'

Since there were very few vacant seats left in the carriage, Sara could hardly deny it. Lifting her head high into the air, she settled herself down into it. Then, to her horror, she found the man had sat himself down into the empty seat beside her.

Oh, this was really too much! she thought furiously. Was she going to have to spend the next ten hours sitting next to some—some tramp?

As if he knew exactly what she was thinking, the man leant a little closer.

'You shouldn't judge people too much by appearances,' he told her, amusement lightening his voice now. 'Underneath this rather outlandish gear, I'm really very civilised.'

Sara didn't even reply. Perhaps if she just ignored him he would get tired of annoying her and go and sit somewhere else.

Only that would be difficult, because there wasn't another vacant seat in the carriage by this time. She couldn't even change seats herself. Anyway, he would probably only follow her, she told herself edgily. For some reason he seemed determined to latch himself on to her.

She still hadn't ruled out the possibility that he was a thief. On the other hand, she had to admit that he didn't *sound* nearly as rough as he looked, and there was the bright glow of intelligence in those deep blue eyes.

He took off his hat, and she saw that his hair was dark blond. It was rather shaggy and in need of a cut, but it was obviously freshly washed, and it gleamed sleekly. And he was clean-shaven, which she supposed was another point in his favour.

That still didn't mean she had to like him, though. Or wanted to spend the next ten hours in his company.

'Do you suppose this would be a good time to introduce ourselves?' he suggested, his blue gaze resting on her lazily.

'I shouldn't think so,' she said in a freezing tone. 'I'm really not in the least interested in knowing who you are.'

He didn't seem in the least put off by her blatant rudeness. In fact, Sara was beginning to wonder exactly what you *did* have to do to make this man lose his temper.

'I'm Lucas Farraday,' he went on, as if she hadn't even spoken. Then, when she didn't introduce herself, he levered himself to his feet and read the label attached to her suitcase. 'Sara Lambert,' he said thoughtfully, as he relaxed back into his seat again. 'Is that Miss, Mrs or Ms?'

'I don't see that's any of your business. Why don't you just go away? I don't want to talk to you.'

He gave an unconcerned shrug. 'Where can I go? The rest of the carriage is completely full.'

'I'm sure you can find a seat in one of the other carriages,' she said irritably.

Just then, though, the train gave a mournful hoot and began to pull out of the station. Lucas Farraday stretched out his long legs, and made himself more comfortable. 'It doesn't look as if I'm going anywhere,' he said cheerfully. 'I'm afraid you'll just have to get used to having me around for the rest of the journey.'

The very thought of it filled Sara with dismay. Since she couldn't physically force him out of the seat, though, she turned her head away and stared pointedly out of the window.

Unfortunately, there wasn't very much to look at. The train was rattling through the outskirts of Lima, and Sara soon got tired of looking at walls plastered with graffiti and overcast skies. If she turned her head back again, though, she would be presented with a clear view of Lucas Farraday; that was even less of a pleasing prospect, so she kept staring fixedly at the shanty town that was spread out on either side of the railway line.

'If you spend the entire journey looking out of the window, you're going to end up with a very painful crick in your neck,' observed Lucas Farraday.

Sara continued to ignore him. If she took absolutely no notice of him, perhaps he would get the message and turn his attention to someone else.

Lima was at last left behind, and instead there were green fields, the occasional small village, and brown hills.

'We should be coming out into the sunshine fairly soon,' Lucas Farraday told her, seeming to assume that Sara would be interested in any snippets of information that he cared to impart. 'Because of the cold current off the coast, Lima remains under a blanket of cloud for much of the year. We'll soon be at Chosica, though, and out of the cloud. Chosica's where a lot of the wealthier people in Lima go if they want to find some sunshine,' he added helpfully.

Sara swung round to face him. 'If I wanted to know that sort of information, I'd read a guide-book! But since I don't care if the sun shines all day or stays stuck behind a cloud, it's of absolutely no interest to me. Go and find someone else to bore with all these irrelevant facts!'

His eyes briefly flickered, and the line of his mouth became a little less relaxed. Was she finally beginning to get through to him? Sara wondered belligerently. She certainly hoped so!

'You're one of the rudest girls I've ever met,' he remarked after a brief pause. Then his long, dark gold lashes lowered a fraction as his gaze slid over her appreciatively. 'You're also one of the most gorgeous,' he went on, in exactly the same tone of voice. 'I don't think I'll give up on you yet.'

Sara had a job hiding her startled surprise. What on earth was he waffling on about? Of course she wasn't gorgeous! She wasn't downright plain, but she was quite certain she was nothing out of the ordinary. Edward occasionally told her that she looked nice, and she supposed that was the word she would have used to describe herself. Nice . . .

"Gorgeous" sounds much better, whispered a tiny voice in her ear. Sara ignored it. She didn't know what this man hoped to achieve by a lot of false flattery, but it certainly wasn't going to get him anywhere.

'Look, I don't know what you're up to,' she stated stiffly, 'but I want you to stop it right now. For some reason, you picked me out at the station, and now you seem determined to keep annoying me. Well, I've had enough. Keep it up any longer and I'll report you to—to—to someone in authority,' she finished rather weakly, realising what a very empty threat it was. There simply wasn't anyone in authority around!

Lucas Farraday's expression changed. 'You don't have to be frightened of me,' he said in an unexpectedly quiet voice.

'I'm certainly not!' she denied indignantly, although not altogether truthfully.

His gaze fixed on her thoughtfully. 'I rather think that you are. What do you think this is? A casual pick-up?'

'I've no idea *what* it is. And I don't really care. I'm not interested in you, or your motives for doing anything.'

'But I'm interested in *you*,' he replied, completely disconcerting her. Then he suddenly smiled. 'Do you know what made me notice you at the station?'

'I've absolutely no idea. And I couldn't care in the least.'

'You looked so totally out of place,' he continued, completely ignoring her last remarks. 'Everyone else just blended into the scene. The locals, going about their everyday affairs, the backpackers setting off to explore another part of Peru—and there you were, sticking out like a sore thumb. You still look out of place,' he commented lazily, his gaze sliding over her. 'All that lovely hair scraped back and tied into place, the smart suitcase instead of something old and practical, and those completely unsuitable clothes——'

Sara looked down at her pleated skirt and neat, matching jacket. 'There's absolutely nothing wrong with my clothes,' she said stiffly. 'I always dress like this.'

'Even on holiday?'

'I'm not on holiday. But if I were, these are the sort of clothes I would wear.'

'Then someone ought to show you how to relax,' he commented.

'Thank you, but I've no desire to walk around looking like a tramp or a drop-out.'

'A drop-out?' he teased lightly. 'That's a rather old-fashioned word nowadays. But I get the feeling that you're not a very modern sort of girl,' he went on reflectively.

'Just because I like to wear nice clothes——' she began heatedly. Then she abruptly stopped. She *wasn't* going to let this man ruffle her, or draw her into any more arguments.

His gaze slid over her clothes again. 'Haven't you ever heard of dressing casually?' he enquired.

She looked rather pointedly at his faded jeans and worn jacket. 'There's a difference between dressing casually and wearing clothes that you wouldn't even send to a jumble sale. Although I dare say they suit your life-style,' she added deprecatingly.

Lucas Farraday still didn't take offence. 'And just what do you suppose my life-style is?' he asked with some interest.

'Well—you're some sort of drifter, aren't you?' she said, clear disapproval in her voice. 'I suppose you just wander around, living as cheaply as you can, and sleeping rough when you run completely out of cash.'

'Not *too* rough,' he said, with a broad smile. 'I like my creature comforts. But don't you think it's a good way of seeing a country properly? Mixing with the people, using local buses and trains, and eating the same food as they do?'

'If you've been eating the same food, you've probably had some fairly spectacular stomach upsets,' Sara commented acidly, remembering all the warnings Edward had given her about only drinking bottled water and never touching food that hadn't been prepared in a hygienic hotel kitchen.

'One or two minor disasters at the beginning,' agreed Lucas Farraday cheerfully. 'But I soon got over them, and I seem to have become immune to the local bacteria now.'

'What are you doing on this train?' She hadn't meant to ask him any questions, because she certainly didn't want him to think she was in the least interested in anything he did. On the other hand, she was beginning to realise that it was going to be very hard—probably quite impossible—to ignore him completely for ten hours. Anyway, she might feel less nervous if she found out something about him. 'Are you going to Huancayo?' she added.

He grinned. 'I wasn't, until half an hour ago.'

Sara looked at him warily. 'What do you mean?'

'I came to the station because one of the hikers at my hotel had left some important papers behind. I wanted to return them to him before he got on the train.'

'And did you find him?'

'Yes, I did. I gave him the papers and was just about to walk away again when I spotted you standing there. My hotel's only a few minutes from the station, so I whipped back there, collected my rucksack, and then came back to catch the train.'

'But—you can't have got on this train just because of me!' she spluttered.

'Why not?' he asked calmly.

'It—it doesn't make any sense.'

'It makes perfect sense to me,' he said in an affable voice.

'You don't even know me!'

'Of course not. But we've got ten hours to get over that small hurdle.'

Sara felt as if she was beginning to flounder out of her depth. It was a new sensation for her, and she didn't like it.

'No one catches a train going to the middle of nowhere because of someone they've seen at the station!'

'We're not going to the middle of nowhere. We're going to Huancayo,' pointed out Lucas Farraday.

Sara didn't like the way he was suddenly using the word "we." Anyway, this whole situation was fast getting out of hand, and she intended to put a stop to it.

'This entire conversation is becoming perfectly ridiculous,' she said, letting the cold tone return to her voice. 'You're obviously having fun at my expense, and I don't like it.'

Lucas Farraday's expression abruptly changed. His eyes became an even darker shade of blue, and his voice purred softly when he finally spoke again.

'If you think that, then I'd better tell you something about myself. I'm thirty-four years old, single, and without any other sort of ties. I've had a couple of mildly serious relationships and quite a few very frivolous ones, but I've never got involved with anyone too deeply. Something's always held me back. All my adult life, I've felt as if I were looking for someone special, and I wasn't ready to settle for second-best. I was willing to wait until that person came along.'

'I'm sure a lot of people would find this very interesting,' Sara replied, not very politely. 'Personally, I don't, since it's nothing at all to do with me.'

Lucas's mouth relaxed into a strange smile. 'I'm afraid that it is. You see, I think you're the one that I've been waiting for, Sara Lambert.'

CHAPTER TWO

SARA thought it was all part of a very unfunny joke. Then she looked at Lucas Farraday's face, and saw that his features had become disturbingly serious.

'That's the most ridiculous thing that anyone's ever said to me,' she got out, choking slightly on the words. Then she cleared her throat and, in a voice that was much clearer and steadier, added, 'I don't want to listen to any more of this. Please don't talk to me any more.'

'How can we get to know each other if we don't talk?' he asked reasonably.

At that, Sara rounded on him, glaring at him furiously. 'I don't *want* to get to know you. Why can't you get that into your thick skull?'

Several heads turned as people sitting near to them heard her raised tone of voice, and she felt the colour sweep over her. Now everyone was looking at her—and it was all this man's fault!

'Perhaps I should have waited a while longer before telling you that,' reflected Lucas. 'But I didn't want you to think this was just a casual pick-up.'

'It isn't a pick-up! It isn't *anything*,' Sara retorted. 'Unfortunately, I can't get away from you at the moment. But once we're off this train I'm going to make very sure I never see you again.'

Lucas merely shrugged. 'We'll see how things work out.' And, before Sara could reply heatedly to that, he went on, 'Here comes the waiter. Do you want some breakfast?'

The last thing Sara felt like at the moment was eating. 'No, thank you,' she got out through gritted teeth, forcing herself to remain polite since the waiter was now within earshot. 'I'll just have some coffee.'

'Wise choice,' Lucas commented. 'This railway line is just about the highest in the world. It hits nearly five thousand metres above sea level at one point.'

Sara was completely uninterested. 'I'm sure that's very thrilling, if you're a railway enthusiast. Personally, all I care about is getting to where I'm going. I don't care if we're five thousand metres above or below sea level.'

'You might, if you get hit by altitude sickness.' Seeing the slightly alarmed look that spread over her face, he gazed at her quizzically. 'You haven't paid much attention to the guide-books, have you? They all warn about altitude sickness. The air gets much thinner at high altitude,' he explained. 'And that affects some people.'

'In what way?' she asked warily.

'Headaches, dizziness, nausea—it knocks some people right out until they adjust to the thinner air, while other people don't get any symptoms at all. And there's really no way of telling if it's going to hit you or not. It just seems to be a question of luck.'

'I suppose *you're* not affected,' she snapped, looking at him with pure dislike.

'No, I'm not,' Lucas agreed cheerfully. 'But since you don't know yet if it's going to affect you or not, it might be a good idea not to eat too much. You'll feel much better with just coffee and a light meal inside you.'

Sara was tempted to ignore his advice and order a huge breakfast. At the last moment, though, she stopped herself. It would be just too embarrassing if she was ill in front of this man.

He was looking at her again now, his brows drawing lightly together.

'Why can't you look out of the window at the scenery, like everyone else?' she said in annoyance, feeling her skin beginning to grow slightly hot under that unfaltering gaze.

'I prefer to look at you,' he replied calmly. 'But you're rather a mystery, Sara Lambert. You're wandering around Peru all by yourself, yet you don't seem to know the first thing about the country. You're dressed quite unsuitably, and you're obviously not enjoying the trip. You've already told me you're not on holiday—so, why are you here?'

'My reasons for being here are absolutely none of your business!'

'Probably not,' he agreed affably. 'But that doesn't stop me from wanting to find out more about you.' His gaze narrowed a fraction. 'Perhaps you're trying to find someone?' he suggested.

His perceptive guess shook her a little. 'Why do you say that?' she said defensively, at last.

'I can't think of any other reason why you'd be going to Huancayo. The town isn't that interesting. Most tourists take this trip just for the train ride. It's meant to be one of the most fascinating in the world, if you're a train buff—which you're definitely not,' he said drily. 'So, if you're going to Huancayo, it's probably to meet someone.' Then his brows drew together. 'A man?' he questioned, in a rather different tone of voice.

'As it happens—no,' retorted Sara. 'But I think you ought to know that I do have a fiancé back in England,' she added. There, she thought with some satisfaction. That should finally put an end to this absurd situation. Perhaps he'll leave me alone now.

To her surprise, though, Lucas seemed to brighten up at her announcement. 'Only a fiancé?' His tone was quite dismissive, as if a fiancé presented no obstacle at all. Then he glanced at her left hand. 'You're not wearing an engagement ring.'

'Edward decided that I should leave it in England,' she replied rather defiantly. 'He thought it would be safer there.'

His gaze immediately swivelled round to fix on her. 'And is that all he's worried about? The safety of your ring?'

Sara bristled. 'Of course not,' she denied indignantly.

'Well, it certainly sounds like it to me,' Lucas growled. 'He's let you come to a strange country on your own, but makes sure he keeps your ring in England. An expensive ring, is it?' he enquired, his tone openly derisive now.

'As a matter of fact, it is,' Sara confirmed sharply. Then, realising that she was only helping to enforce this man's low opinion of Edward, she added immediately, 'But that had absolutely nothing to do with it. Edward isn't with me because I've come to South America on a—on a personal matter.'

'If you can't share a personal matter with your fiancé, who can you share it with?' Lucas pointed out very reasonably.

Sara didn't even bother to reply. Her relationship with Edward was nothing at all to do with this irritating man. She certainly didn't intend to discuss it with him any further.

She turned her head away and began to look out of the window again. The sun was shining brightly now, illuminating the immense hills that loomed around them. The railway track seemed to cling precariously to the hillside most of the time, and her stomach sank a couple of inches every time the train rattled over one of the precarious bridges that littered the route.

To her relief, Lucas remained silent. In fact, when ten minutes had passed and there still hadn't been a word out of him, she risked a quick glance in his direction and discovered that he had gone to sleep.

She had no idea how anyone could sleep so soundly on this noisy, rattling train, but he was clearly managing it without any problems. He looked completely relaxed, sprawled out on the seat with his long legs spread out in front of him and his battered hat covering his eyes to keep out the light.

For a few moments, she allowed herself to study him, taking stock of this man who had so arrogantly barged into her life. He wasn't exactly good-looking, but he had the kind of face that you would certainly find it hard to forget. Sara just wished that she had never seen it in the first place. She didn't need someone like Lucas Farraday hanging around, causing her endless trouble and irritation. At the moment, she already had more than enough of that.

Lucas didn't open his eyes again until the train shuddered to a temporary halt at a small station. He pushed his hat back and then levered himself to his feet.

'Where are you going?' asked Sara in surprise.

He grinned at her. 'Not far, sweetheart. You don't get rid of me that easily. I'm just going to get something to eat.'

'Is there a café at the station?' She frowned. 'Surely the train won't stop long enough for you to get a meal?'

His grin broadened. 'There isn't a café, and the train only stops for a few minutes. The local tradespeople come down to meet the train, though. I'll be able to buy whatever I need from them.'

'You're going to buy food from some stall?' she said, genuinely shocked. 'You'll go down with food poisoning!'

'I told you, my stomach's acclimatised itself to all the local germs and bacteria. Anything I can get for you?' he added helpfully.

'No!' she said, with a small shudder. 'Anyway, the hotel's given me a packed lunch.'

Lucas looked unimpressed. 'Soggy sandwiches? You'd enjoy some of the local stuff a lot better.'

'But not the after-effects! I'll stick to my sandwiches.'

He returned just a few minutes later with some pastries that smelt delicious, and some kind of fruit that was large and green.

'What on earth's that?' she asked, staring at it with some fascination.

'Maracuya. It tastes slightly sour, and it's very refreshing. Want to try some?'

What Sara would really have liked was one of the pastries. Just the smell of them was making her mouth water. Instead, though, she took out her sandwiches and daintily began to eat them, pretending that they tasted far better than they looked.

The hills became mountains as the train climbed higher into the Andes. After he had eaten, Lucas went back to sleep again, and Sara was grateful for that.

It meant that, for a while at least, she could pretend that he wasn't even there.

Although she was vaguely aware that they were passing through some fairly spectacular scenery, she wasn't in the mood to appreciate it. Instead, she began thinking about Clarissa Lambert again. What was she going to say to her, when they finally met up in Huancayo? Sara had no idea. She hadn't rehearsed any speeches. She just hoped she could hold on to her temper. She didn't want to get involved in any embarrassing slanging matches. On the other hand, she was so furious over the loss of her home and everything that was precious to her that she knew it was going to be very hard to stay cool and controlled.

'If you keep frowning like that, you'll end up with wrinkles,' murmured Lucas. His eyes had flickered open again, and their dark blue gaze was now fixed on her.

'Oh, stop making personal remarks and go back to sleep!' she said in annoyance. To her surprise, he did just that.

The train rounded a sharp bend a little further on, and Lucas's relaxed body slid closer to hers, so that he was actually resting against her. Sara waited for him to move. When he didn't she gave him a sharp jab.

'Stop lolling all over me,' she ordered, as he woke up.

Unperturbed, he eased himself away from her. 'Do you always get uptight over physical contact?' he enquired with some interest.

'Of course not. I just don't like strangers draping themselves all over me,' she snapped back at him. Angrily, she turned away from him and ran her fingers over her hair, which was beginning to escape from the confining clips that held it in place. She was starting to get a headache, and she just wasn't in the mood for any more battles of words with Lucas Farraday. In fact, she would be extremely pleased if he got up and walked away, and she never saw him again.

At that point, the train entered a tunnel and she gave a small gasp as darkness closed in on them. They had been through other tunnels, but only short ones. This one just seemed to go on and on, and the lack of light made her begin to feel curiously disorientated. Then a cool hand closed over her own, and just held it in a soothing gesture. Sara automatically began to snatch her fingers away, but the grip of Lucas's hand tightened and didn't let go again until they were out of the tunnel.

As soon as they were back in the daylight, Sara felt much better. Then she rounded on Lucas. 'There was no need for that,' she said hotly. 'I was perfectly all right. Or were you just looking for an excuse to paw me?'

The expression in his dark blue eyes briefly altered. Then he studied her thoughtfully. 'You've got a lot of hang-ups, haven't you?' he remarked at last. 'But don't worry, we'll work our way through them.'

'We certainly will not!' When he merely grinned, she shook her head in total exasperation. 'Oh, what have I got to do to get through to you?' Angrily, she looked around the carriage and saw there was an empty seat at the far end. Someone must have either got off or be sitting outside on the steps, getting some fresh air.

'I'm changing seats,' she said with some determination, and she began to get to her feet.

She didn't get very far, though. As soon as she stood up, she suddenly felt dizzy and had to sit down rather abruptly again.

'It looks as if the altitude's beginning to get to you,' said Lucas, with brisk sympathy. 'You'd better sit still for a while.'

'I'm fine,' she insisted stubbornly. 'It was the swaying of the train, that's all.' She began to haul herself out of the seat again, but didn't get very far. Her legs just sort of gave way under her, and she sat down heavily, gasping a little.

'Wait here a moment,' Lucas instructed. Then he got up and disappeared down the carriage.

Sara couldn't do much else. She slumped in her seat and felt totally miserable. Her head ached, she felt slightly sick, and she just couldn't escape from this man who seemed to be trying to take over her life.

Lucas returned in a couple of minutes with a man who was carrying a tank of oxygen. The nozzle of the tank was stuffed under Sara's nose, and then she could hear the hiss of air being released.

'Breathe deeply and evenly,' instructed Lucas. 'It should make you feel slightly better.'

After a couple of minutes, Sara was aware of a small improvement in her condition. The man with the oxygen tank gave a small nod of satisfaction, and then moved away to help another of the passengers who was looking slightly green around the gills.

'Who's he?' muttered Sara. 'The railway's equivalent of the flying doctor?'

'They always carry oxygen on this route, for people who are affected by the altitude,' Lucas told her. Then he looked at her more closely. 'You still don't look too good. Why don't you try and sleep for a while?'

'The seat's too uncomfortable.'

'You can use my shoulder as a pillow,' he offered.

'No, thank you,' Sara refused stiffly. Then she closed her eyes and told herself she would feel much better once they reached Huancayo—and once she could get away from Lucas Farraday.

The afternoon seemed to drag by as the train trundled on through the mountains. The high peaks gradually gave way to softer, more rolling country. And after the magnificent bleakness of the mountains the land gradually became more fertile. There were fields of maize, groves of eucalyptus, and bullocks slowly ambling along. Sara saw very little of it, though. Her eyes ached even more when she opened them, and so most of the time she kept them shut.

By the time the train finally reached Huancayo, she felt as if she had been on it for ten weeks instead of ten hours. She got stiffly to her feet and was glad to find that her legs were supporting her again—although only just. They still felt dangerously wobbly, and she didn't know how she was going to carry her suitcase and bag.

Lucas solved the problem by hauling them down from the rack and carrying them off the train for her, along with his own rucksack. He carried the extra weight with ease, and still managed to prop her up with a spare hand as she tottered dizzily out of the station.

'Do you have a hotel booking?' he asked her.

'I've got the address here, in my bag.' She fumbled around, looking for the piece of paper that the clerk of the hotel in Lima had given her. Finally, she found it. 'Here it is.'

'We'd better take a taxi,' Lucas decided. 'I don't think those legs of yours are going to get you very far.'

'There's no need for you to come any further,' she insisted, as a dusty car responded to a signal from Lucas and roared to a halt in front of them. 'I'm starting to feel better now. I can manage perfectly well on my own.'

Lucas simply ignored her. He shovelled her luggage into the car, propelled her into the back seat, and settled himself in beside the driver. He then proceeded to haggle over the fare in what sounded like fluent Spanish.

'Oh, pay him whatever he wants,' muttered Sara wearily. 'I just want to get to the hotel.'

'We'll pay him a fair amount, plus a tip,' said Lucas firmly. Then he launched into another flood of Spanish. A couple of minutes later, he seemed to strike some sort of bargain with the taxi-driver and, to Sara's utter relief, they got under way.

It wasn't far to the hotel. Lucas carried in the luggage and, after Sara had registered, asked the clerk for a room for himself.

At that, Sara spun round. 'You can't stay here!'

'Why not?' he enquired reasonably.

'Because you can't,' she flung at him, her tone suddenly becoming stormy. 'Go and find some other hotel!'

'But this one suits me very well,' came his calm reply. 'I'm not tramping around Huancayo trying to find somewhere else.'

'I don't want you here.'

'Yes, you do, sweetheart,' he said with a disarming smile. 'It's just that you haven't realised it yet.'

The conceit of the man infuriated her. Who did he think he was, walking into her life and coolly assuming that she would be pleased to have him there? She had a fiancé, and a future that was already very carefully planned out. She didn't need or want someone like Lucas Farraday.

On the other hand, she didn't see how she could stop him from registering at the hotel. The only thing she could do was to walk out herself, and find somewhere else to stay. She was too tired and had too much of a headache to do that, though. Anyway, Clarissa was staying here. That was the reason she had *come* to Huancayo, to see her stepmother. It would be crazy to disrupt all her plans because of a complete stranger.

She turned back to the clerk. 'Can you tell me which room Mrs Clarissa Lambert is staying in?' she asked, keeping her voice low and hoping that Lucas couldn't hear. She might have had to share a train journey with him, but she certainly didn't want him to know all about her private affairs.

'Mrs Lambert?' the hotel clerk said politely, in excellent English. 'I'm afraid she checked out at the beginning of the week.'

Sara just stared at him in utter dismay. 'Checked out?' she repeated numbly. 'But they told me at the hotel in Lima that she was staying here.'

'Yes, she *was* here for a few days,' confirmed the clerk. 'But she has left now.'

It was just too much for Sara. Quite suddenly, she couldn't seem to cope with this latest setback, not on top of the endless, exhausting travelling, and the upsets and emotionally draining days that had gone before. Something inside her just seemed to collapse, as if the will-power that had kept her going had broken down into small, shattered pieces.

'Something wrong?' enquired Lucas, from just behind her. His voice was unexpectedly gentle and, for some reason, it struck a painfully raw nerve. She actually quivered, as if he had physically touched her.

She began to say something, but the words wouldn't come out. For some inexplicable reason, she found herself thinking of the day of her father's funeral. There had been such an awful lump in her throat that she had felt as if she were choking, but she hadn't been able to break down in the tears that would relieve it. She hadn't cried during all the long days since, either. Everyone had commented on how well she had taken it, had admired her for the way she had coped with it all. Only she didn't seem to be coping any more. Finding that Clarissa wasn't here was somehow the last straw. To have travelled all this way for nothing, to have to face the journey back home again with everything still unresolved——

It was as if she had suddenly run out of whatever it was that had kept her going. She tried again to speak and explain that she was all right—that she just needed a couple of minutes to get over this attack of tiredness and depression that had swooped over her and nearly knocked her off her feet. Instead, though, to her astonishment—and total embarrassment—she burst into tears.

Sara hardly ever cried—and never in a public place. She just couldn't stop, though. She stood there with the tears streaming down her face and great hiccuping sobs erupting from her, and *nothing* she did would put an end to them. It was the most awful thing that had ever happened to her. She knew that everyone in the hotel reception area had to be staring at her, and she wanted to sink through a huge hole in the floor and never come up again.

Then she realised that someone had put their arms around her. Instinctively, she began to push them away. It was too much of an effort, though, and in the end she leant weakly against a hard, warm body until the sobs finally petered out through sheer exhaustion.

'Come on, I'll take you up to your room,' murmured Lucas's voice in her ear.

The world began to swim back into focus as the tears slowly started to clear from her red, sore eyes. Lucas? She had been leaning against Lucas Farraday?

With an enormous effort, she shrugged herself free of him.

'I'm all right,' she somehow got out in a choked voice.

'Of course you aren't,' he replied firmly. Then he took hold of her arm, and led her towards the stairs.

Sara didn't have much choice except to go with him. His grip on her arm was light but surprisingly forceful. Anyway, she was a very long way from being totally in control of herself again. Her head ached, her legs felt horribly weak, and she was absolutely terrified that she would start crying all over again if just one more small thing went wrong today.

When they reached the first floor, Lucas led her along a short corridor and then stopped outside one of the doors. He opened it and, when she didn't move, gave her a small push which propelled her inside.

Sara vaguely noted that the room was very modestly furnished, but looked clean and comfortable. Then she caught a glimpse of her reflection in the mirror on the far wall.

Her eyes were swollen and rather bloodshot while, in contrast, her face was deathly pale. A hank of her black hair had completely escaped from the clips, and was tumbling over one shoulder, and the rest of it was threatening to escape down in a black cloud at any moment.

'Oh,' she moaned out loud. 'I look awful.'

'If you're starting to worry about your appearance, you're obviously feeling a little better,' remarked Lucas, with a faint smile. 'And you don't look awful. You look gorgeous. Dishevelled and very tempting. If you weren't in such a state, I might not be able to resist the urge to kiss you.'

He took hold of her arm again, and steered her across the room.

'What are you doing?' muttered Sara.

'Putting you to bed.' Then, as her eyes suddenly flared in alarm, he gave her a reassuring grin. 'Don't worry. Much as I'd like to, I'm not going to lay a finger on you.'

'I need to wash first,' she mumbled. 'And get out of these clothes——'

'You need to sleep,' he replied firmly. Then he gave her a gentle shove which, in her present condition, was all that was needed to send her tumbling on to the bed.

It felt marvellous to be lying down on a soft mattress. Sara closed her eyes, and gave a small sigh of relief. Then she immediately opened them again. Was Lucas Farraday still there? She didn't want him hanging around, watching her while she slept.

She found he was looking down at her with a rather odd look on his face. When he saw that she was still awake, though, his expression altered, and she couldn't tell what he was thinking.

'You don't feel safe with me in the same room?' he said, with a rather crooked smile. 'Then I'll leave you on your own. I'll be just across the corridor, though, if you need me.' He seemed about to leave but, at the last moment, he turned back, bent over, and kissed her very lightly on the forehead. 'Goodnight, sweetheart,' he murmured in a slightly husky voice. Then he walked out of the room and closed the door behind him.

Sara wanted to rush over and lock the door, to make sure that he couldn't come barging back in again whenever he felt like it. She didn't have the energy to get off the bed, though. She couldn't even manage to keep her eyes open for more than a few seconds.

And her last thought, as she fell asleep, was that her forehead still tingled lightly where Lucas Farraday had kissed it.

CHAPTER THREE

SARA slept deeply and dreamlessly. It was the first really good night's sleep she had had for ages, and when she finally opened her eyes again she felt clear-headed and refreshed.

The room was full of daylight, so she guessed she had slept late. She sat up, and ran her fingers through the long, dark fall of her hair, which had freed itself from the last of the clips during the night. Then she sat very still for a moment as her fingers touched her forehead.

Embarrassment swept right over her again as she remembered that shameful scene in the reception area. What on earth had made her break down and cry like that, in front of everyone? She had hung on to her self-control for so long. If she had had to cry, she should at least have waited until she had reached the privacy of her own room.

It must all be part of the altitude sickness, she told herself at last. There was no other possible explanation. And since she felt much better this morning, with her headache and the dizziness almost gone, there shouldn't be any danger of a repeat of that awful episode.

She sorted out a towel, her toiletry bag and a fresh change of clothes, and then set off to look for the bathroom. She found one at the end of the corridor and, although it was fairly basic, at least it had piping hot running water.

By the time she returned to her own room, she felt more or less ready to face the world again. She slapped on some make-up to disguise the last faint traces of puffiness around her eyes. Then she decided to go down and see if she could get a late breakfast.

She had just opened her door when Lucas Farraday appeared out of the room opposite.

For a moment, Sara had trouble in meeting his eyes. He had seen her as few people had, at a total disadvantage and with all her defences in complete disarray. Then she reminded herself that it really didn't matter. After today, he would be out of her life for good. She would never see him again.

His dark blue gaze was moving over her with a clear gleam of disappointment.

'You've scraped your hair back again,' he remarked. 'Why don't you leave it loose?'

'Because it's much more practical to keep it tied back,' she replied. Then she was immediately annoyed with herself for even bothering to answer his question. What business was it of his how she wore her hair?

'A girl of your age shouldn't want to look practical,' Lucas pointed out. 'You should want to look beautiful.'

'And I don't, with my hair like this?' she enquired acerbically.

'Of course you do,' he answered promptly. 'I can't think of anything you could do to yourself to make you look ugly. But with your hair loose, you'd look a little less strait-laced—more approachable,' he finished softly.

But Sara didn't want to look approachable—and particularly not to this man. Although she was loath to admit it, in some ways she found him highly disturbing. He was so—well, so unlike anyone she had ever met before. So unlike Edward——

'Coming down to breakfast?' invited Lucas.

Sara wanted to refuse, but didn't because she was so hungry. She had eaten next to nothing yesterday, and her stomach would start positively growling soon if she didn't get some food.

As they sat down at one of the tables in the tiny dining-room, Lucas looked at her.

'Are you still interested in meeting up with Clarissa Lambert?'

Sara's head jerked up. 'What do you know about Clarissa?' she demanded.

'Nothing at all. But I heard you asking the clerk for her room number yesterday. I figured that she had to be the reason you'd come all the way to Huancayo. Who is she?' he asked, with some interest. 'A relative of some kind?'

'She's my stepmother,' replied Sara briefly, after a long pause. She hoped that would satisfy him, but his blue eyes began to brighten, as if he was pleased that she was finally beginning to open up to him a little.

'Are the two of you close?'

'Hardly!' Sara exploded. 'I haven't seen her for twenty-two years. I was just two and a half when she walked out on my father.'

Lucas began to look even more interested. 'Tell me more about your stepmother,' he encouraged her.

'There's not much else to say,' she said stiffly. 'I don't know anything about her, except that she's travelling around Peru at the moment, getting ideas for the knitwear she designs.'

'And you're finding it very hard to catch up with her?'

'I don't see why the wretched woman can't just stay in one place,' muttered Sara. 'Unless she knows I'm here,' she added, her face darkening as she considered that possibility. 'Perhaps she's trying to get away from me.'

'Why would she want to do that?' enquired Lucas. His eyes gleamed. 'I know that if you were chasing me. *I* wouldn't be trying to get away from you.'

Sara shot him a filthy look. 'If you're just going to joke about this——'

'I'm not,' he assured her. 'But you seem to take life so very seriously all the time. Don't you ever take time out for fun?'

'There hasn't been much chance of any fun lately,' she said in a low voice.

Lucas's eyes narrowed. 'Had a rough time?' he said more softly. 'Was that the reason for all those tears last night?'

She lifted her head defiantly. 'Certainly not! That was just the altitude sickness. It made me feel ill and out of sorts.'

'High altitude affects people in a lot of different ways,' Lucas said consideringly. 'But it doesn't make you cry. At least, not the way you cried last night. It takes something a lot more personal to do that. What was it?' he questioned her in a rather different tone of voice. 'A lousy love-affair? No,' he said, without even giving her time to answer. 'You haven't had any love-affairs lately. Perhaps not ever. Then how about the death of someone close to you?' he guessed, with another flash of that perceptiveness that was so beginning to unnerve her.

'My father died,' she said briefly. Then her eyes suddenly blazed at him. 'And as for not having any love-affairs lately—that's a perfectly ridiculous thing to say. I'm engaged,' she reminded him angrily. 'And Edward and I are very close.'

'You might be engaged,' Lucas agreed in a completely unperturbed voice. 'You might even be close to this Edward that you keep rattling on about. But you're certainly not having a love-affair, Sara.'

His voice turned her name into a caress, and a light shiver ran over the surface of her skin.

'You're wrong about that,' she told him sharply.

'Am I?' His eyebrows lifted a fraction. 'Somehow, I don't think so. But don't let's argue about it. Tell me about your father.'

'What's there to say?' she said in a flat tone. 'He died.'

'Were you close?'

'No.'

Her blunt answer didn't seem to surprise him. 'Was that his fault, or yours?'

Her eyes flew wide open. 'His!' she said, far more heatedly than she had intended. Then she bit her lip. 'His,' she repeated, in a duller voice. 'He wasn't interested in me. In fact, he wasn't interested in anyone—except Clarissa,' she finished with some bitterness.

'Your stepmother?' Lucas gave a brief, puzzled frown. 'But you said she walked out on him.'

'She did. And he spent the next twenty-two years waiting for her to come back.' The words began to tumble out of Sara, and she couldn't seem to stop them. All the resentment, the frustration of trying to love someone who didn't want to be loved in return—at least, not by her—suddenly burst out in a rapid torrent. 'Everyone knew that Clarissa wouldn't be coming back,' she said angrily. 'Everyone, except for him. He just wouldn't let go. He wouldn't accept she had gone forever. He never tried to get a divorce, or even a legal separation. I suppose he thought that, if he hung on to their marriage, he would somehow still be holding on to *her*.'

'He couldn't have been a very happy man,' observed Lucas.

'He was obsessed! He was in love with someone who probably forgot all about him the moment she walked out of the door. He certainly never forgot her, though. He didn't even change his will. Twenty-two years without her, and yet he still wanted to give her absolutely everything he had!'

'Ah,' said Lucas, with new understanding. 'I think we're finally getting down to the heart of it. Your father left everything to your stepmother, instead of you,' he concluded, quite correctly. 'So you've come hotfoot to South America to find her. What are you going to do?' he asked, with a faint frown of disapproval. 'Try to force her to give everything back to you? Threaten to contest the will unless you get a fair share?'

'And why not?' demanded Sara, thoroughly annoyed by his sudden change of attitude. For some reason, she had assumed he would be on *her* side. Instead, he was looking positively censorious, and clearly thought she was doing the wrong thing.

'I think that your father had the right to leave his possessions to whomever he pleased,' Lucas stated firmly.

Her mouth dropped open. 'How can you say that? I've lived in that house for twenty-four years. It's my home. I love it. She was there for just eighteen months—*eighteen months*,' she repeated in utter indignation. 'And yet, now it's hers! And not just the house. Everything that's *in* it's hers. Well, as far as

I'm concerned, she's got no right to any of it. And she'll be very sorry if she doesn't see things in the same way,' she warned grimly.

Lucas looked as if he was seeing a side of her that he didn't particularly like. Sara didn't care, though. This man's opinion of her was of absolutely no consequence, as far as she was concerned.

'Are you planning to marry this Edward of yours in the near future?' he asked at last.

The change of subject flummoxed her for a moment. Then she rather defiantly lifted her head. 'We were planning on getting married next year. But now my father's died, there's every chance we'll be bringing the date of the wedding forward.'

Lucas growled something under his breath that she didn't quite catch; then he frowned again. 'If you're planning on marrying Edward, why are you so determined to hang on to your old home?'

'Because I've a right to it! And because——' She gave a brief, frustrated gesture with her hands. How could she possibly explain to this man how much her home meant to her? Now that her father had gone and she was completely alone in the world, it was all she had to hold on to. It represented security, safety, something that was *hers*. Only it wasn't hers, she reminded herself grimly. Not yet. Right at this moment, it legally belonged to Clarissa.

'Why shouldn't I want to hang on to it?' she demanded rather belligerently, at last.

Lucas shrugged. 'I thought you were planning to start a new life with Edward?'

'I am,' she insisted promptly.

'Then why are you trying so hard to hold on to the past?' he enquired, with a questioning lift of one dark blond eyebrow. 'If Edward means so much to you, then you shouldn't need anything else.'

Sara opened her mouth, and then closed it again. He had neatly pushed her into a tight corner, and she didn't know how to get out of it.

'I don't have to explain my reasons to you,' she said finally, in a tight voice. 'Anyway, Edward is one hundred per cent behind me in this.'

'Then why isn't he here, with you?'

'Because——' Sara began. Then she stopped and glared at him. 'I've had enough of this,' she said furiously, jumping to her feet. 'I don't have to answer all these questions. None of this is any of your damned business!'

A couple of people turned to look at her, and she realised she had been shouting. She closed her eyes in abrupt dismay. This was the second public scene she had made in less than twenty-four hours. What on earth was the matter with her?

Lucas caught hold of her wrist and firmly pulled her back into her chair.

'Stop getting so worked up,' he said placidly. 'You'll only get indigestion. Eat your breakfast, and then we'll discuss where you ought to go from here.'

'I can't eat,' she muttered.

It was true. Her stomach was rumbling with emptiness, but she couldn't swallow a single mouthful of the food on her plate.

'Of course you can,' he encouraged her gently. 'Try just one mouthful, eat it slowly, and forget about everything else for a while.'

His voice was unexpectedly soothing. Sara could almost feel the tension easing out of her rigid muscles as his dark tones washed over her. Much to her amazement, she found herself doing exactly as he had instructed. Getting the first mouthful down wasn't easy, but it gradually became less difficult after that, and in a remarkably short time her plate was completely empty.

'More coffee?' he offered. When she gave a subdued shake of her head, he refilled his own cup and then sat back and looked at her. 'Then perhaps you'd like to know where you can find your stepmother?' he suggested.

Her head jerked up. 'How can you possibly know where to find Clarissa?' she demanded.

'I asked the hotel clerk if he knew where she had gone,' he replied calmly. 'It turns out that he made all the arrangements for her.'

'Then where is she?'

'Cuzco.'

'Cuzco?' Sara repeated blankly. 'But that's a couple of hundred miles from here!'

'Probably more,' replied Lucas. 'And the only way to get there from Huancayo is by bus. It takes at least a couple of days, and it's a journey that I wouldn't recommend. But if you return to Lima, you can fly from there to Cuzco. It's only about an hour by plane. That's if you're still determined to find your stepmother,' he added.

What Sara really wanted right now was to go home and forget all about this wild-goose chase. She was already sick of South America, the last person in the world she wanted to see was Clarissa Lambert, and she was thoroughly tired of Lucas Farraday hanging around, organising her life for her and being so damned interfering!

She knew that she couldn't go back, though. It would be mad to come all this way and spend so much money without getting some sort of result. Like it or not, she had to see this through to the end.

'I suppose you've also got the address of Clarissa's hotel in Cuzco?' she said, with a touch of angry sarcasm.

'She isn't staying in a hotel,' Lucas answered in an unperturbed voice. 'She's rented a house for a couple of weeks.' He gave her an unexpected smile. 'That's good news, as far as you're concerned. It looks as if she's planning on staying in the same place for a while.'

'Then I suppose I'd better head back to Lima,' she reluctantly decided. 'The sooner I get that flight to Cuzco, the better. Do you know the time of the next train?'

'Yes. It's tomorrow morning.'

'Tomorrow?' she echoed in disbelief. 'But there's got to be a train before then!'

Lucas shook his head. 'You'll either have to spend another day in Huancayo, or take the bus to Lima.'

'Then I'll take the bus,' she said promptly.

'A long journey on a Peruvian bus can be quite an experience,' he warned drily. 'I think you'd be far better off waiting for the train.'

'I can cope with a bus journey,' she flashed back immediately. 'What time does it leave?'

Lucas glanced at his watch. 'It was scheduled to leave quarter of an hour ago. But don't panic,' he went on with a grin, as she shot an angry glare at him. 'They hardly ever leave on time. You've got time to pack, have another cup of coffee, and still catch the bus.'

But Sara wasn't taking any chances. She paid her bill, ran up to her room, packed in record time, and was back in the hotel lobby in a matter of minutes.

Fast as she had been, though, Lucas, was still there before her. Moreover, he was carrying his rucksack and wearing that awful hat which she hated so much.

'Where do you think you're going?' she demanded at once.

He gave a relaxed shrug. 'I'd have thought that was fairly obvious. I'm returning to Lima.'

'Not with me, you're not!'

'I don't quite see how you're going to stop me,' came his unruffled reply. 'The bus is public transport. You can't stop me from catching it.'

'But I don't want you trailing around after me. I'm really sick of it! Why can't you just stay here, in Huancayo?'

His eyebrows lifted in gentle surprise. 'Why on earth would I want to do that?'

'I have no idea,' she retorted in a blaze of irritation. 'Why did you come here in the first place?'

'To be with you, of course,' he replied, to her complete consternation. 'I thought I'd already explained that.'

'You did, but I didn't believe you. I *still* don't believe you. No one takes a ten-hour train journey to the middle of nowhere because of a stranger!'

Lucas gave her a strange smile, which made the delicate hairs on her skin stand straight up on end. 'You're not a stranger to me, Sara. It's just that I'm having a little trouble convincing you of that fact. Perhaps the bus journey back to Lima will give me the opportunity that I need,' he added reflectively. 'It'll certainly give us plenty of time in each other's company.'

'Oh, no, it won't,' Sara flung back at him furiously. 'I might not be able to stop you getting on the bus, but I certainly don't have to sit next to you!'

'Unless we get a move on, neither of us will be getting on the bus at all,' he pointed out. 'Although it usually leaves late, it won't sit in the bus station all morning.'

Sara grabbed hold of her case and was just about to stride off when she realised she didn't have the slightest idea where to go.

'This way,' said Lucas, with a grin. His fingers closed lightly round her arm, and pointed her in the right direction.

Sara immediately shook herself free. 'You always seem to be finding some excuse to touch me,' she accused angrily.

'Don't you like to be touched?' he enquired with some interest. Then he shot a sly glance at her. 'Doesn't Edward touch you?'

'What Edward does has absolutely nothing to do with you!' she snapped back at him. 'Anyway, I don't think it's necessary to keep touching all the time.'

Lucas's dark blue eyes grew thoughtful. 'Then Edward *doesn't* touch you,' he mused. 'At least, not very often. What's wrong with the man?'

Sara's own eyes became positively stormy. 'There's nothing at all wrong with Edward! Just because he knows how to behave like a gentleman——'

'I think you'd have a lot more fun with someone who didn't behave like a gentleman,' Lucas murmured. Then, before she could fling another furious reply back at him, he quickened his step. 'We'd better shift, or the bus will leave without us.'

He walked so fast that Sara had quite a job keeping up with him. She certainly didn't have any breath left to continue the argument. Perhaps that had been his intention, she told herself with a dark scowl. All men liked to have the last word on a subject!

They arrived at the bus station just as the bus was beginning to pull out. Lucas flagged it down by the simple expedient of standing in front of it. As it shuddered to a halt, though, Sara stared at it in dismay.

'It's completely full.'

'Not quite.' Lucas hauled her on board, and they shuffled their way to the very back of the bus, where there were just two vacant seats next to each other.

'That's a bit of luck, isn't it?' he commented, his eyes gleaming as he settled himself down beside her.

Sara didn't even bother to reply. As far as she was concerned, it wasn't lucky at all. In fact, it was like the train all over again. Hours and hours of travelling ahead of her, and every minute of it spent in the company of Lucas Farraday. She knew that it was quite impossible for him to have arranged it, so it meant that the man must just have the luck of the Devil.

That didn't mean that she had to talk to him, though. In fact, she didn't even have to acknowledge his presence. She ignored all his attempts at conversation and, after a while, he seemed to get the message and shut up. There was rather a warning gleam in his eyes, though, and she had the feeling that she was finally beginning to get under his skin.

Good! she said to herself, with some satisfaction. Because he had certainly been annoying her since the first moment she had set eyes on him!

After a couple of hours, Sara was definitely regretting that she had ever set out on this journey. The bus was hot and crowded, and didn't seem to have any kind of springs. On top of that, she was beginning to wonder if they were ever going to reach Lima. The engine coughed and spluttered every time it had to climb up a gentle incline, and didn't even run very well when it was going downhill.

Lucas turned to her. 'Are you going to give me the silent treatment all the way to Lima?' he asked, the amusement back in his voice now.

'I'm going to do my very best,' she replied with some determination.

'If you talked to me, it would help to pass the time.'

'I can think of far more interesting things to do.'

'Such as?' he enquired lightly.

'Sleeping,' she replied promptly. 'I'm going to take a nap.' With that, she pointedly closed her eyes, and was determined to keep them shut for as long as possible. It was about the only way she could blot out Lucas Farraday's face.

Although she hadn't actually intended to, she fell asleep. When she eventually opened her eyes again, it took her a while to figure out where she was. Blinking dozily, she looked round the crowded bus, and then at the unfamiliar scenery outside the window. South America, she thought to herself rather groggily, as everything slowly began to filter back. The bus to Lima——

Then she realised that she was curled up rather comfortably against the person sitting next to her. Growing scarlet with embarrassment, she quickly sat up very straight. 'Sorry,' she muttered apologetically. Then she remembered *who* she was sitting next to, and the colour in her cheeks flared even brighter. Lucas Farraday—and there was an infuriatingly satisfied grin on his face, as if he had thoroughly enjoyed every moment that they had been in such close contact.

'Why didn't you wake me up?' she said hotly.

One dark gold eyebrow lifted. 'Whatever for?'

'To stop me from slumping all over you, of course!'

'But I like it when you slump over me,' he purred. 'If you want to, you can do it all the way to Lima.'

Sara turned her head away and didn't deign to answer. This man was getting more and more infuriating. If she couldn't shake him off soon, she might end up hitting him!

Never mind, she comforted herself. You'll be free of him once you get to Lima. He certainly won't follow you to Cuzco. For one thing, he wouldn't be able to afford the air fare!

The bus jolted on through the day, and although Sara was still tired she didn't dare let herself go to sleep again. At one of the stops that the bus made, she bought a bottle of soft drink and some pastries stuffed with meat. Edward's warnings about eating local food echoed in her ears, but she was so hungry that she had to eat something. She thoroughly enjoyed the pastries, but couldn't help worrying about any possible after-effects.

'Don't look so apprehensive,' murmured Lucas in her ear, as she swallowed the last mouthful. 'They won't poison you.'

'Edward said that I should be very careful of locally cooked food,' she said defensively.

'And do you always take notice of everything that Edward says?' he asked in a slightly bored tone, as if he were tired of hearing even the mention of Edward's name. 'Can't you think for yourself?'

That gibe hit her rather hard, for some reason. 'Of course I can,' she shot back at him fiercely. 'But I— I love Edward,' she rushed on, suddenly feeling ridiculously embarrassed at having to say those highly personal words out loud. 'Of course I'm going to listen to whatever advice he gives me.'

'And does Edward love you?' enquired Lucas.

His highly impertinent question made her swivel round in her seat and glare at him. 'He certainly does! We're engaged,' she said heatedly, and wished that she was still wearing her ring, so that she could thrust it under his nose.

Lucas looked unconvinced. 'If you were engaged to *me*, I wouldn't let you go roaming around a strange country on your own.'

'Edward knows that I can cope perfectly well.' Which wasn't the exact truth, because she had never admitted to Edward how very nervous she had been at coming all this way by herself, or how much she had secretly wished he would just drop everything and insist on coming with her. 'Anyway, he's a very busy man,' she went on defensively. 'Some people have to work for a living.' She shot a scathing look at Lucas. 'They can't spend their time just drifting around, wasting their lives and living off other people's charity.'

His mouth tightened just a fraction. 'And you think that's what I do?'

'Of course it is! Or are you going to pretend you're a top industrialist just taking a couple of months' sabbatical?' she added with some sarcasm. 'Because if you are, save your breath. I'm not going to swallow that one! I can see what you are by simply looking at you.'

The line of Lucas's mouth didn't relax, and his eyes rested on her very coolly.

'You're very quick to judge people by their appearance.'

'It's usually a good guide to someone's character.' Her gaze drifted pointedly over his well-worn clothes. 'No one who could afford to buy something better would dress like that.'

'You think a dark suit and white shirt would be suitable for travelling rough around this country?'

'Of course not. But there's a difference between dressing casually and looking like a reject from a jumble sale.'

For just a moment, she thought she had gone too far. His eyes noticeably darkened, and his fingers tapped together in a warning rhythm. In truth, Sara had no idea why she was being so extremely rude. Normally, she would never have dreamt of talking to anyone like this. It was just that he got her back up, she told herself defensively. Making all those remarks about Edward—and none of them were true. Of course they weren't!

Lucas sat back in his seat and looked at her. 'Well, if we're judging people by appearances, perhaps it's time I made a few observations about you.' His gaze slid over her with what seemed, to Sara, like unnecessary thoroughness. 'Neat, unobtrusive clothes,' he remarked at last. 'Perhaps a little too unobtrusive. Almost as if you don't want anyone to notice you. Are these the sort of clothes that you wear for work, Sara?'

'Yes, they are,' she said stiffly. 'And I don't see that there's anything wrong with them.'

'They would be perfect—for someone twice your age,' Lucas responded. Then, before she could say anything, he went on, 'If you dress like this for work, my guess is that you work in an office of some kind. A solicitor's, perhaps—or some kind of financial institution?'

'I work in a bank,' she admitted with some reluctance, rather annoyed that he had been able to pinpoint it so accurately.

'They've given you time off, to look for your stepmother?'

'I've taken a week of my annual leave, with the option to take a second week, if I need it.'

'And what if you can't find Clarissa and get all this cleared up in two weeks?'

'I will be able to,' she insisted. 'I've *got* to.'

Lucas's eyes narrowed. 'It really is important to you, isn't it?'

'Of course it is! I'd hardly have come all this way if it wasn't.'

'You like to have everything in your life organised?'

'Yes. No. Oh, you couldn't possibly be expected to understand,' she finished impatiently.

'I understand that you're very uptight,' he said softly. 'And that you shouldn't be expected to cope with something like this on your own.'

He was doing it again, she thought with some annoyance. Having a sly dig at Edward, insinuating that he ought to be here with her.

She decided that she didn't want to listen to any more of it. She closed her eyes, and was determined to keep them shut for the rest of the journey. Except that, this time, she definitely wouldn't go to sleep. She didn't want to wake up and find she was draped all over Lucas again!

The bus seemed to jolt and rattle its way on forever. Its only good point was that it did finally reach Lima, quite late in the evening.

Stiff and aching in every bone and muscle, Sara levered herself out of her seat, took hold of her case, and stumbled off the bus. It was far too late now to catch a flight to Cuzco, which meant an overnight stay in Lima. She decided that she might as well return to the hotel that she had stayed in before, and began to look around for a taxi.

One roared over to them a minute later, in response to a loud whistle and a vigorous gesture from Lucas. He opened the door for Sara, and then smiled at her disarmingly.

'Since you've decided I'm short of money, you won't mind if we share it?' he said, with a bright gleam from his eyes. Then, before she had a chance to object, he slid in beside her.

Lima by night was no more impressive than Lima by day. She was sure the city had its good points, but either she had missed them, or she just wasn't in the mood to appreciate them. She didn't even bother to look out of the window, and heaved a sigh of relief when they finally reached the hotel. She was itching for a bath and then a long sleep in a soft bed.

It wasn't until Lucas began to follow her into the hotel that she began to become suspicious.

She rounded on him with furious eyes. 'Are we going to have to go through this all over again?' she demanded. 'It's getting really boring, trying to get rid of you.'

'Then why not stop trying?' he suggested easily.

'Why don't *you* go and find your own hotel?' she retaliated. 'I'm getting really sick of finding you a couple of inches behind me every time I turn round.'

'You're just upset because you're tired. Why don't you go straight up to bed, have a good sleep, and leave me to sort things out for you?'

'What sort of things?' she demanded.

'For a start, I'll book your plane ticket to Cuzco,' he offered.

'I can do that for myself,' Sara insisted firmly.

'Of course you can. But you're just about asleep on your feet. Let me do it for you.'

'Why are you being so helpful, when I've done nothing except be rude to you all day?' she said suspiciously.

His expression became very hard to read. 'I think that you know the answer to that,' he said, after a brief pause. 'And if you don't, then it's too late—and you're too tired—to go into it right now.'

'You talk an awful lot of nonsense,' she muttered. At the same time, she avoided looking at him. Something a bit odd seemed to happen to her whenever she stared directly into his dark blue eyes. 'But if you really want to run around booking my plane ticket, I suppose I can't stop you,' she added, rather ungraciously. 'If you manage to get a ticket, just leave it at the desk. I'll pick it up in the morning.' When he didn't move, she glared at him. 'What are you just standing there for?'

'Waiting for a goodnight kiss?' he suggested, a faint smile touching the corners of his mouth.

'Then you'll wait a long time,' she slung back at him heatedly. 'I don't kiss anyone.'

Lucas's eyebrows shot up. 'Not even Edward?'

'Will you shut up about Edward?' she howled back at him. Then she grabbed hold of her case and hurriedly beat a retreat up the stairs before she lost her temper completely, and made yet another scene in a hotel lobby.

Despite everything, she had a good night's sleep, and woke up in the morning feeling a lot more refreshed. When she checked at the desk her plane ticket was waiting for her. There was just time for a quick breakfast, and she kept glancing round as she made her way to the dining-room. She was certain Lucas would suddenly pop up and confront her at any moment. There was no sign of him, though, and he wasn't waiting for her in the dining room. Sara gave a small frown. Where was he?

Then she realised that she shouldn't be worrying about where he had gone. She just ought to be highly relieved that she seemed to have finally got rid of him.

She ate quickly; then she collected her luggage and went out to the taxi that was waiting to take her to the airport. Despite her determination not to think about Lucas, she found herself automatically turning round, still half expecting to see him appearing at the very last moment.

'It looks as if he's finally got tired of annoying you,' she muttered to herself as she clambered into the taxi. Then she wondered why that made her feel just a little bit peeved.

The airport terminal was crowded, but she somehow managed to get to the right gate at the right time. She was just about to hand over her luggage when a very familiar voice murmured in her ear.

'Take it with you on the plane. Peruvian airlines have got an absolute talent for sending your luggage in the opposite direction to wherever you're going.'

The sound of Lucas's voice didn't make her jump. It was as if she had been subconsciously expecting it.

'I suppose you've come to say goodbye?' she said, in a voice that didn't sound altogether like her own. 'Well, you needn't have bothered. Although I suppose I ought to thank you for getting my ticket.'

'It was a pleasure,' Lucas said, his gaze drifting over her with some absorption, as if they had been separated for several days instead of just a few hours. 'And there's no need for you to say goodbye. I'm coming with you to Cuzco.'

CHAPTER FOUR

SARA realised that she wasn't surprised. Part of her seemed to have known all along that something like this would happen. That didn't mean she had to like it, though.

'When you didn't show up at the hotel this morning, I thought I'd finally got rid of you,' she said with some irritation. 'I should have guessed you'd turn up, though. You seem to be getting some weird kick out of following me around.'

'I wasn't at the hotel because I had to go to the bank,' Lucas replied pleasantly.

'What did you do? Rob it, to get some money to pay for your ticket?' she enquired sarcastically.

Instead of taking offence, Lucas merely grinned. It really was remarkable how difficult it was to make this man lose his temper.

'No, I withdrew the money in the usual, fairly orthodox way,' he informed her. Then he gently pushed her forward. 'Let's get moving, or we won't get on the plane.'

As she had expected, he had booked himself a seat right next to hers. She sat down, and then scowled darkly. This was getting beyond a joke. She had been so sure she would finally leave Lucas behind once she flew to Cuzco. Yet here he was, still dogging her footsteps. What if he took this whole mad situation to its ultimate conclusion, and followed her all the way back to England? At the very thought of it, her eyes flew wide open. How could she possibly explain the presence of this tall, blond-haired man to Edward? It would be bad enough if he ever found out she had travelled all over Peru with a total stranger. But if that same stranger turned up in England Edward would be bound to get suspicious. Any reasonable man would!

She had to admit that the thought of Edward being jealous gave her just a small twinge of satisfaction. There were times when she felt he rather took her for granted, assuming that she would never be interested in any other man—and that no man, except for him, would be interested in her.

Then she immediately felt guilty. She ought to be *pleased* that Edward was so sure of himself, and of her. That was one of the things she liked about him, wasn't it? His solidness, and the sense of security that he gave her?

'Thinking about Edward?' asked Lucas in an interested voice.

The unexpected interruption of her thoughts—and the accuracy of Lucas's guess—made Sara jump.

'How did you know that?' she demanded.

'Because you were frowning,' he replied. 'You always frown when you're thinking or talking about Edward. Do you suppose that's significant?' he went on thoughtfully.

'I think that you're just making it up,' she retorted. 'I'm sure that Edward never makes me frown.'

'And what else doesn't he make you do?' asked Lucas in a much softer voice.

She stared at him uneasily. 'What do you mean?'

'Does he make your skin quiver when he touches you? Do his kisses make your bones melt?' Lucas's dark blue gaze bored down into hers. 'Do you ache to go to bed with him, Sara?' he finished in a low, husky undertone.

Sara felt herself shiver. Then she made a huge effort to pull herself together.

'Don't be so disgusting,' she said in a cold voice.

Lucas continued to look at her in a way that made her nerve-ends curl in a most peculiar manner.

'Do you think it's disgusting to want all those things from someone that you love?'

'Whether I do or not, I'm certainly not going to discuss it with you,' she replied, her tone still deliberately freezing.

To her relief, Lucas released her from that dark blue gaze and settled back in his seat.

'For a girl of twenty-four, you've got a lot of things still to learn,' he observed.

'I'm sure that Edward will be more than happy to teach them to me,' she replied stiffly.

His gaze returned to rest on her gently. 'I'm not sure that Edward can teach you anything at all.'

She glared at him furiously. 'And you think that you can?'

'I'm sure of it,' he replied comfortably. 'But I think you need a little more time before you come round to the same way of thinking.'

'About a million years,' she flung back at him. 'And I might need even longer than that!'

She sat back in her seat and deliberately closed her eyes.

'Going to sleep this early in the morning?' enquired Lucas. 'Or are you just trying to shut me out?'

'I'm trying to pretend that you don't even exist!'

'But I'm still going to be here when you open your eyes, sweetheart.'

'For how long?' she demanded.

'How long am I going to be around? Maybe for the rest of your life,' he replied, to her complete consternation. 'I've waited a long time for you, Sara Lambert. I'm not going to let go of you now that I've found you.'

Something in his voice disturbed her far more than she cared to admit. Although he had kept his voice deliberately light, she had the feeling that he meant every word that he had said.

Slowly, she opened her eyes again. 'All right,' she said, with some reluctance. 'Let's talk about this.'

'What is there to say?' he replied, sounding very relaxed again now. 'I've always felt as if I've been waiting for one particular person. When I saw you standing at that station, I knew *you* were that person.'

'But that's quite ridiculous,' she said, trying hard to keep her own voice both steady and reasonable. 'You can't just look at someone and know something like that. You didn't even know me. You *still* don't know me.'

'I think I do,' came Lucas's unperturbed reply. 'Oh, not all the small details. But I know all the important things.'

Sara shook her head. 'I'm sorry, but I can't believe any of this.'

'Why not?'

'Because this kind of thing doesn't happen to someone like me.'

'Someone like you?' Lucas repeated enquiringly.

'Someone—ordinary.'

Surprise immediately showed in his blue eyes. 'Is that how you think of yourself? As ordinary?'

'Well—of course,' she said, beginning to feel distinctly embarrassed now. She didn't like it when conversations became this personal.

His dark blond eyebrows drew together in the beginnings of a frown. 'Who told you that you were ordinary? Edward? Or does he just make you *feel* ordinary?' he growled.

'Edward doesn't have anything to do with this,' she snapped back sharply. 'I know for myself what I am.'

'Do you?' His gaze drifted over her. 'You've got beautiful black hair. Perfect skin. Huge green eyes fringed with the longest damned lashes I've ever seen. If you bought some decent clothes, wore your hair loose instead of scraping it back with all those clips, and just loosened up a little, you'd turn just about every man's head. Even looking the way you do right now, you certainly turned mine,' he added softly.

'I'm not interested in turning heads,' Sara insisted. 'I'm perfectly happy with the way I look. And so is Edward.'

'Then Edward's a fool. A man should want the woman he loves to look as gorgeous as possible.'

'If you say just one more word about Edward, I shall get extremely angry,' she informed him in a freezing tone.

Lucas looked as if there were a whole lot more he wanted to say, but he obviously got the message because he remained silent for quite a long while after that. Sara was both pleased and relieved. She didn't want to discuss Edward with Lucas ever again.

It was some time later before Lucas turned to her again. 'Take a look out of the window,' he advised.

Sara turned her head; then she gave a small gasp and immediately wished that she hadn't. They seemed to be flying perilously close to an extremely large mountain. Although the views were stupendous, she decided she would rather be seeing them from a much safer distance.

'Isn't the pilot a—a little close?' she said with a gulp.

Lucas grinned. 'Some of them like to fly a lot nearer than others. This one obviously likes to skim pretty close and let the passengers get a good look. The mountain's called Salcantay,' he went on. 'Fairly impressive, isn't it?'

'I suppose so,' she got out in a slightly strangled voice. 'How long before we get to Cuzco? *If* we get to Cuzco,' she added nervously.

'Not long now.'

'Thank heavens for that! I've tried Peruvian buses, trains and planes, and I can't say I'm too thrilled by any of them.'

'Perhaps we'll try donkeys next time,' suggested Lucas.

Sara didn't like the way that he kept saying 'we.' It implied that they were going to be seeing a lot more of each other, and she wasn't at all sure how she felt about that.

Not sure? she asked herself a moment later, in pure astonishment. Of course you're sure! You want to get rid of him, and never see him again.

Yet it was strange how used she was getting to having him around. Strange, and a little unnerving. She shot a quick sideways glance at him, and then immediately coloured as she found him looking straight back at her. Very hurriedly, she switched her gaze away from him and back to the breathtaking— and slightly stomach-churning—views from the window. She might be disturbed by the nearness of that mountain, but she edgily realised that she was even more disturbed by the closeness of Lucas Farraday.

After they had landed at the airport, they had to jostle their way through the crowds. As usual, though, Lucas managed to whistle up a taxi in a remarkably short time. He gave the driver the address of the house that Clarissa Lambert had rented. Then, as Sara had expected, he climbed into the taxi beside her.

'How am I going to explain you to my stepmother?' she said in some exasperation.

'You don't have to explain me to anyone,' Lucas replied calmly. Then his eyes glinted. 'On the other hand, perhaps you could introduce me to your stepmother as "Edward,"' he suggested. 'I'm sure I'd make a perfect fiancé.'

'I don't think you'd make a perfect anything! And I don't want to hear you even mention Edward's name again.'

His dark blue gaze flashed wickedly. 'I'm certainly willing to forget all about him—if you are.'

Sara lifted her head. 'I shall never forget Edward,' she said with some dignity.

Lucas immediately looked sympathetic. 'Good heavens, is he *that* dull? It's funny how really boring people stick in your memory.'

Sara ignored him, and instead concentrated on her first sight of Cuzco. It was quite different from Lima, and she had the feeling that this was a much more friendly city. The stone buildings were a mixture of Spanish and Inca architecture, with both styles often combined in the same building. The Inca stonework was very distinctive, with large, cut blocks of stone beautifully fitted together in plain walls, while the later Spanish influence was much more ornate. Every street corner seemed to have a ruined temple or palace, and Sara found herself becoming unexpectedly enchanted with this unique city.

'They say that Manco Capac, the first Inca emperor, came here with his four sisters from the land of the sunrise,' Lucas told her, noticing her growing fascination. 'He brought with him a wedge of gold, and as they travelled he pushed the wedge into the ground at regular intervals. When they reached this place, the wedge of gold inexplicably disappeared right into the ground. Manco Capac decided that this must be the centre of the earth, and built his city here.'

A few minutes later, the taxi rattled its way out into a large square. Here, crowds of tourists mixed with Peruvian Indians, most of them women wearing very full skirts, bright knitwear, and light coloured hats with darker bands around the crown.

'The Plaza de Armas,' said Lucas. 'This was the heart of Cuzco when it was an Inca city, and it's remained the centre of the modern city.'

Sara gave him a faint smile. 'Cuzco doesn't look very modern to me.'

'It's certainly kept a great deal of its charm,' Lucas agreed.

The taxi swerved out of the square again, shot down a couple of side streets, and finally screeched to a halt. Then the driver turned and said something to Lucas in rapid Spanish.

'This is it,' said Lucas, turning to Sara. He dug some money out of his pocket, but as he began to hand it over to the driver Sara caught hold of his arm.

'I should be paying the fare,' she insisted.

Lucas shot an amused smile at her. 'Do you think I can't afford it?'

'I've no idea,' she said. And that was the truth. She was beginning to suspect that Lucas wasn't the penniless drifter that she had originally assumed him to be. She still didn't know quite *what* he was, though.

'I'm the one who wanted to come to Cuzco,' she reminded him. 'I should be paying all the expenses.'

'Stop arguing, and get out of the taxi,' he said affably. 'The driver wants to be off, to collect his next fare.'

Since the driver was revving the engine impatiently and looked as if he might set off with her still in it, if she didn't get out fairly quickly, Sara scrambled out. The taxi noisily shot off, leaving her and Lucas standing outside a small house in the narrow side road.

Sara's brows drew together in a light frown. 'Why do you suppose Clarissa's rented a house, instead of staying in a hotel?'

'Perhaps it's the only accommodation she could get,' answered Lucas. 'Cuzco's very popular with tourists, and the hotels fill up pretty fast. Quite apart from it being a unique city in its own right, you also get the train from here to Machu Picchu, the lost city of the Incas. Since that's a "must" for most people visiting Peru, the tourists head for Cuzco in their droves.'

Sara was only half listening now, though. She had already begun to walk through the small archway that led through to a tiny stone-flagged courtyard. Then she stopped again. The front door was just a few steps ahead, but her legs didn't seem to want to move.

'Last-minute nerves, now you're about to come face to face with your stepmother?' said Lucas perceptively.

'Of course not,' she lied. 'I'm just—just getting my breath back, that's all. Cuzco's a high-altitude city,' she told him. 'All the guide-books warn you to take it very easy for the first couple of days.'

'Knocking on a door isn't too strenuous,' Lucas commented. 'But I'll do it for you, if you like.'

For once, she didn't argue with him, although she didn't know why she was suddenly behaving like such a coward. She certainly wasn't *scared* of a showdown with Clarissa Lambert. Why should she be? she argued with herself defiantly. She was the one who was in the right. It was Clarissa who had to back down, and admit that Sara's father had had no right to give away his daughter's inheritance.

All the same, her nerves gave an unexpected leap as the door slowly opened in response to Lucas's vigorous knock.

The girl who opened it, though, most certainly wasn't Clarissa. She was young and dark-haired, and looked almost as nervous as Sara. She said something in soft Spanish, and seemed very relieved when Lucas immediately answered her in the same language.

A fairly long conversation followed, and Sara became more and more frustrated at not being able to follow any of it. She supposed that she should have learnt a few basic phrases of Spanish before coming to South America, but at the time it had hardly seemed worth it. She had only planned to stay for two or three days. Just long enough to convince Clarissa that she had no right to Sara's home, or all the personal possessions that went with it.

Instead, she had ended up tramping over what seemed like half of Peru. Not only that, but she had somehow managed to get involved with Lucas Farraday, who seemed to see her as some sort of girl of his dreams.

At last, the conversation came to an end. 'Well?' questioned Sara impatiently. 'What did she say? Have we come to the wrong house?'

'No, this is the right address,' confirmed Lucas.

'Then where's Clarissa? Not out sightseeing for the day?' she said with a sudden sinking of her heart, dreading another long delay before she could finally confront her stepmother.

'She's visiting a couple of the nearby villages,' Lucas told her. 'Your stepmother seems to have an absolutely inexhaustible appetite for local crafts. By the way, this is Teresa,' he went on, gesturing towards the dark-haired girl. 'She's a sort of housekeeper. She does all the shopping and cooking, and whatever other odd jobs need doing.'

Sara smiled politely at Teresa, and then immediately turned back to Lucas.

'When will Clarissa be back? Later today?'

'Not exactly.'

'When, then?'

'Not until the end of the week.' He shrugged philosophically. 'She left yesterday and, according to Teresa, was planning to be away four or five days.'

'Oh, I don't believe this!' exploded Sara in exasperation. 'What on earth am I meant to do now?'

'Why not stay here for a few days, enjoy the sights of Cuzco, and just relax?' suggested Lucas.

'I don't want to sit around doing nothing!' she yelled at him. 'I want to see Clarissa, sort out this mess my father's left behind, and then go back home.'

'Your father didn't leave a mess,' Lucas pointed out with infuriating precision. 'As far as he was concerned, his will was perfectly clear and specific. He wanted everything he had to go to Clarissa. *You're* the one who won't accept that, and who's trying to overturn his decision.'

Put like that, it made her seem like some sort of monster. A greedy, grasping daughter who wanted to get her hands on everything that she could. And it wasn't *like* that, Sara insisted to herself. How could this man possibly paint her in such a black light?

'Why not come inside?' suggested Lucas. 'Then you can work out where you want to go from here.'

But Sara didn't want to set a foot inside her stepmother's house.

'No,' she said stubbornly. 'I'll find a hotel to stay in.'

'Chances are they're all full,' he warned. 'And I'm sure Clarissa would want you to stay here.'

'I don't give a damn what Clarissa wants!' she hurled back at him. Then, to her horror, she could feel the warning prickle of tears at the back of her eyes.

Oh, please, she prayed silently, don't let me cry again in front of this man.

As if sensing the enormous struggle that was going on inside her, Lucas walked over and put one arm around her shoulder. Then he firmly shepherded her inside the house. She heard him say something to Teresa, and the girl disappeared through a doorway at the end of the narrow, dark hall.

'She's gone to make us some tea,' he told her. 'Come on through, into here.'

Sara found herself being gently shunted into a nearby room, which was unexpectedly light and spacious. It was very simply furnished, and had a homely feel to it.

Lucas's arm was still around her, and she had the feeling that he had no intention of letting go of her. She tried to move free of him, but his other arm came up and stopped her from moving more than a couple of inches.

'Let me go,' she muttered.

'Not just yet. You're too upset. What you need,' he mused thoughtfully, 'is something to take your mind off things. Would you like me to kiss you?'

'No,' she said sharply.

'Sure? I promise that it would stop you thinking about Clarissa—in fact, about all your problems.'

Sara was a little horrified to find that she was actually tempted. It would be so nice to forget about everything, let it all just drift away...

With a small jerk of her head, she stopped herself from even thinking about it.

'I never kiss anyone,' she reminded him in a frigid voice. 'Except for Edward,' she amended rather hurriedly.

'Forget Edward,' Lucas murmured.

'I can't——'

'Yes, you can,' he instructed. 'Just for a few seconds.'

Then he stopped talking altogether, and let his mouth do the persuading. His lips were cool and firm. Sara couldn't help comparing them to Edward's, which always seemed a little damp and awkward, as if he didn't know quite what to do with her mouth once he was in close contact with it.

Lucas certainly knew, though. He explored gently but very thoroughly, and was obviously finding a deep pleasure in this first intimate contact.

Sara knew perfectly well that she ought to be pulling away from him, but she was finding it astonishingly hard to do so. It was so *relaxing*, just standing there and letting Lucas's lips move over hers in that gentle and undemanding way. No fumbling, no slightly embarrassing pauses as they altered position or paused for breath. It all seemed so easy, so natural, as if they had been kissing like this for years.

Then Sara became aware that Lucas was beginning to want much more than just a kiss. With a small jerk of shock, she pulled back from him, and felt the colour rise in her face.

He seemed entirely unperturbed by the response of his body, though. He bent his head for another kiss, although this time there was no other contact between them.

Sara meant to turn her head away, but didn't. These kisses of his could become addictive, she thought to herself with a small pang of fear. And when he began to ease his body closer to hers again, her nerves suddenly jumped and she backed away, her eyes becoming guarded.

'Is that far enough for now?' Lucas queried softly. 'Perhaps you're right,' he went on drily. 'Teresa will be back with the tea in a few minutes, and I don't think we should shock her too much before we've even moved in.'

'You—you can't move in,' she croaked.

'Of course I can,' he replied easily. 'We'll have separate rooms, of course,' he went on. His eyes briefly gleamed. 'Unless, of course, you'd prefer it otherwise.'

Sara was beginning to recover a little now. 'No, I wouldn't,' she shot back. 'And you shouldn't have— shouldn't have——'

'Shouldn't have kissed you?' he suggested. Then his eyes glittered even more brightly. 'Shouldn't have wanted you?' he went on in a much huskier tone of voice.

His words made her go positively scarlet. She wasn't used to talking about such things with such openness.

'Why were you so shocked at my reaction?' he went on thoughtfully. 'I've already explained how I feel about you. Did you think that didn't include a physical attraction?'

Sara was saved from having to answer by the opening of the door. Teresa glided in, put the tea-tray down on the table, and then tactfully withdrew again.

'I like that girl,' grinned Lucas. 'She knows when she's not wanted.' He poured the tea and handed her a cup, but when Sara went to take it she found her hand was shaking.

'It's the altitude,' she said defiantly. 'It's making me feel a bit—a bit wobbly.'

'Of course it is,' he agreed suavely, and she knew perfectly well that he didn't believe a word of her explanation.

Sara managed to drink her tea, and felt slightly better afterwards. And now that she had begun to calm down again she realised that she didn't really have much choice except to stay here, in this house Clarissa had rented. At least it meant that she would finally get to see Clarissa when she returned from her trip.

That didn't mean that she was ready to let Lucas move in as well, though.

'I think it would be much better if you found a hotel room for yourself,' she said, in what she hoped was an extremely firm voice.

'But I'd much prefer to stay here,' Lucas said, with the sort of smile that would have charmed a whole flock of birds down from the trees.

'I can't let you do that,' Sara replied, with a decisive shake of her head. 'This isn't even my house. I can't let some stranger move in.'

'But I'm not a stranger.' Lucas was still smiling, but there was a sudden edge to his voice, as if her words hadn't at all pleased him.

'I don't know a thing about you, except your name,' Sara pointed out.

His gaze locked on to hers, making her want to squirm. 'Oh, I think that you know quite a lot about me,' he said softly. 'But if you want a few factual details, I'll be quite happy to supply them.'

'All right, then,' she said slowly. 'You can start by telling me what you do for a living. You're *not* a drifter, are you?'

'I never said that I was,' he reminded her. 'You're the one who gave me that label.'

'Well, that's hardly surprising, considering the way you're dressed,' Sara replied defensively.

'What made you change your mind and decide that I wasn't a—what did you call me?' he grinned. 'A drop-out?'

'Something like that,' she admitted. 'For a start, you had too much money. You forked out the fares for trains, buses and taxis without batting an eyelid. And when you bought that plane ticket, that just about clinched it. Either you had a lot of cash in hand, or you'd robbed a bank! I figured it must be the former. Whatever else you might be, I don't think you're dishonest.'

'That must be the first compliment you've ever paid me,' he said drily. 'But you're right, I'm not a drifter. And I'm not short of cash. I came to South America for a few weeks' break—a prolonged holiday, I suppose you'd call it. And I like to travel like this, because I think it's the best way to see a country and meet the people.'

'Why not go to Europe, if you wanted a holiday?' she asked curiously.

Lucas gave a small shrug. 'I've seen most of Europe. I thought I'd try somewhere different.'

'You've had a pretty long holiday,' she commented. 'Didn't you have any trouble getting the time off from work?'

'No, I didn't. You see, I own the company.'

Sara blinked in surprise. 'You own——?' She recovered slightly. 'What sort of company is it?'

'It's called Farraday Aviation. We deal mainly in air freight, although we're beginning to branch out into charter work. We operate out of a small airfield in Essex.'

She looked at him doubtfully. 'Is your company doing well? Can you afford to take so much time off?'

'I can't afford not to,' Lucas said wryly. Then, seeing her puzzled look he went on, 'I've spent much of the last year fighting off a takeover. One of the larger companies decided that they'd try and swallow us up. We're OK now, but I had to work day and night for a long time, to make sure I could hold on to my company. In the end, I just about worked myself to a standstill. The doctor told me that if I didn't take a complete break, there was a chance I'd physically crack up.' He smiled ruefully. 'It seemed like good advice, so I decided to take it.'

'Aren't you worried about leaving your company to run itself? What if some other emergency comes up?'

'The company's in a very secure position right now. And I ring them every couple of days, to make sure they're managing all right without me.' His mouth twitched. 'It seems that they are—which isn't very flattering.'

'When are you going back to England?'

'Probably in another week or two. Even the most interesting holiday begins to lose its sparkle after a while.'

'Your family must miss you while you're away.' She knew that she was fishing for more information about him and, from the gleam in his eyes, so did he.

'My mother and my two sisters won't miss seeing me for a few weeks. Although they're probably missing being able to indulge in their favourite hobby.'

'What's that?'

'Trying to fix me up with a marriageable girl-friend.' His mouth curled into a slow smile. 'I can't seem to make them understand that I like to find my own women.'

'And do you find very many?' Sara enquired with some acerbity.

'Enough,' Lucas said placidly. 'And there's no need to go that bright colour or look so disapproving,' he went on comfortably. 'I've already told you that I've never met anyone I wanted to get seriously involved with on a long-term basis.'

'I probably wasn't listening,' she said, keeping her voice as detached as she possibly could. 'After all, it's of absolutely no interest to me.'

'Then why are you asking all these questions?'

'I'm—I'm just making conversation,' she prevari-cated. 'And that's *all*,' she finished fiercely.

Lucas didn't follow it up any further, and she was grateful for that. Instead, he stretched his lean limbs, and then prowled across the room, as if he were sud-denly beginning to feel rather cooped-up.

'How about a walk around Cuzco?' he suggested. 'And we could get something to eat, while we're out.'

'All right,' she agreed at once. And when he glanced at her, clearly surprised by her unexpected amena-bility, she smiled sweetly back at him. 'And while we're out, we'll try a few hotels—to see if they've a spare room for you.'

Lucas growled something under his breath, but didn't argue with her. Instead, he headed for the door, leaving her to trail along behind him.

As soon as they left the house, Lucas began to stride off purposefully.

'Have you been to Cuzco before?' Sara asked a little breathlessly, as she scurried to keep up with him.

'No,' he replied briefly.

'Then how do you know where we're going? You haven't got any map.'

'But I do have a perfect sense of direction.' They turned one last corner while he was talking, and he gave a nod of satisfaction. 'Here we are. The Plaza de Armas.'

Sara gazed with fascination at the large square, which she had had little more than a glimpse of earlier as they had rattled through it in the taxi. It was packed with tourists, local people and peddlers, but was large enough not to seem overcrowded.

'That's the cathedral,' Lucas told her, pointing to the far side of the square. 'Very large, very impressive and, like a lot of churches around here, it's actually built on the ruins of an Inca palace. But the church of La Compania is far more beautiful.' He swung her round so that she was facing it, and Sara had to admit that the church, with its soaring towers and baroque façade, was quite something. 'At night, it's often illuminated,' Lucas went on. 'We'll make sure we see it before we leave Cuzco.'

He was doing it again, she thought with some annoyance. Using the word ''we'' all the time. Surely he realised by now that she wasn't free? That she was going to spend the rest of her life with Edward?

For some reason, that thought unaccountably depressed her. 'Let's get something to eat,' she said, rather too quickly. 'Then we'll try and find you a hotel room.'

They had lunch at one of the cafés in the square. Sara knew that she ought to be enjoying herself, sitting in this lovely square and watching the people of Cuzco going about their everyday affairs. Her spirits remained low, though, and didn't improve during the afternoon when they tried at least a dozen hotels and were told the same thing in all of them. Fully booked—no rooms available at all.

Lucas looked predictably smug. He didn't actually say 'I told you so,' but Sara knew perfectly well that he was thinking it.

'It looks as if I'm going to have to stay overnight,' he said cheerfully, as they at last made their way back to Clarissa's house.

'If I had any sense, I'd shove you out and let you sleep rough,' she muttered.

'But you're not going to, are you?'

'I suppose not.' She had no idea why she was being so soft, though. Lucas Farraday was more than capable of looking after himself. She didn't *have* to offer him a bed for the night. 'You'll have to go first thing in the morning, though,' she warned. 'If you can't find somewhere to stay, you'll just have to get the plane back to Lima.'

'Oh, we'll both be leaving in the morning,' he told her easily.

Her eyebrows shot up. 'Leaving? For where?'

'Machu Picchu.'

'Machu—what?'

'Machu Picchu,' he repeated patiently. 'The lost city of the Incas—I mentioned it earlier.'

'You might have mentioned it, but I don't remember it—probably because I'm not interested,' she retorted. 'And I certainly don't want to see it.'

'Of course you do,' Lucas replied calmly, but very firmly. 'Everyone who comes to Cuzco visits Machu Picchu.'

'I've come here to see Clarissa, not to tramp around all the tourist sights!'

'But Clarissa isn't here,' he reminded her. 'So we might as well make use of the couple of free days we've got on our hands.' He moved towards the door. 'The train leaves early, but I'll wake you up in good time.'

'Don't bother,' she flung after him, but it was already too late. He had left the room, closing the door firmly behind him, as if to cut off the arguments he knew she was going to throw at him.

'Overbearing man!' Sara muttered under her breath. 'Arranging my life for me, always hanging around, *interfering* all the time.'

But the really scary thing was that she was finding it harder and harder to fight him. She was almost getting used to him being around—having someone to lean on when she needed support, or to make decisions when she was too tired and confused to make them for herself.

And those kisses——

She gave a small shiver. How had this happened? How on earth would she ever explain it to Edward? Perhaps it would be better not to mention it at all. She didn't like keeping secrets from Edward, but she had the feeling that he would never understand about Lucas Farraday. She didn't even understand it herself.

One thing was certain, though. She wasn't going to any lost city of the Incas with him in the morning. He would just have to go by himself.

The thought of Lucas being away for a whole day made her feel ridiculously empty inside.

What nonsense! she told herself crossly. You don't *need* him. And soon he'll be out of your life altogether. It'll be just you and Edward again.

But that thought made her feel even more low. In the end, she decided that the altitude was beginning to get to her again, bringing on a sudden bout of depression. All the guide-books recommended rest, so she would go to bed and get in a few extra hours of sleep. That should cure her.

And tomorrow she would have a very quiet, restful day. She definitely *wasn't* going to tramp all round some site with the outlandish name of Machu Picchu!

CHAPTER FIVE

SARA woke up in the morning with a small groan. Someone was knocking on her door, and she didn't want to get up yet. She didn't even want to open her eyes for another couple of hours.

'If you're not out of that bed in five minutes, I'll have to come in and drag you out,' warned Lucas from the other side of the door. 'Although I think that I'd rather enjoy that,' he went on, a note of relish creeping into his voice.

'Go away,' mumbled Sara. 'I don't want to go to Machu whatsit.'

'You'll love it, once you're there.' He rapped on the door again. 'Five minutes, Sara,' he repeated. Then she heard his footsteps moving away.

She huddled under the sheets, and wished that she was back home. South America might be fascinating, but she just wasn't in the mood to appreciate it. Anyway, it had a lot of drawbacks, as well. And right at this moment she counted Lucas Farraday as one of them!

On the other hand, did she really want to stay in Cuzco all by herself? Wouldn't that be even more depressing than being dragged round some ancient Inca ruins?

Sara let out a deep sigh, then she slowly crawled out of bed. She supposed she would have to go. Quite apart from anything else, she didn't want to give Lucas any excuse for coming into her bedroom. Although he seemed very easy-going and laid-back for most of the time, there was a sharp brightness in his eyes now and again which warned of an underlying alertness. And those kisses yesterday had clearly told her that he was interested in more than just her mind!

She trudged along to the bathroom, and had a quick shower which alternated between scalding hot and freezing cold, without ever hitting a happy medium. At least it woke her up, though. By the time she returned to her bedroom to find some clean clothes, her eyes were wide open and she felt completely clear-headed.

When she opened the wardrobe, though, she found her clothes had gone. For a moment, she just stared blankly at the empty shelves and hangers. Then she realised that a thief must have broken in during the night, and she gulped hard. It wasn't at all pleasant to think of a stranger prowling round her room while she had been asleep.

She pulled her bathrobe tightly around her, and then hurried out the bedroom. She finally found Lucas in the kitchen, making himself some coffee.

'We've been burgled,' she told him in a rather shaky voice.

'Have we?' To her annoyance, he didn't seem particularly perturbed. Didn't anything get this man into a flap? 'What's missing?' he went on.

'My clothes! And probably some other things. I haven't had a chance to check everything yet.'

'Don't bother,' he said calmly. 'It's only your clothes that have gone. And they haven't been stolen. I've simply removed them.'

Sara stared at him in disbelief. 'You've what?' she managed to splutter at last.

'Removed them,' he repeated, in a relaxed tone. 'But don't worry. I went out late yesterday, and bought you some replacements.'

Sara ran her fingers through the long, dark, tousled strands of her hair. 'I don't believe any of this,' she muttered. 'I think that either you're going a little crazy, or I am!'

'Both of us are perfectly sane,' said Lucas, with a grin. 'And I had a very good reason for removing your clothes.'

'Then I'd very much like to hear it,' she retorted.

'High-heeled shoes and neat little suits are very suitable for wearing to work. They're a lot less suitable for travelling around South America, but I suppose if you don't mind being very uncomfortable, you can just about get by in them. But they're definitely not the sort of thing you can wear to a place like Machu Picchu. I knew it would take all day to persuade you of that, though, so I decided just to whip them away.'

'Well, you can just whip them straight back again,' she said furiously. 'I'm not going to have you dictate what I wear!'

His own voice remained quite placid. 'Why not be sensible about this? You're going to spend the day tramping round a lot of ruins, and walking over some pretty uneven ground. You'll need to wear casual clothes and footwear for that.'

'I won't, if I don't go!' she flung back at him.

'If you don't go, you'll miss seeing one of the most spectacular and famous sites in South America,' Lucas pointed out. 'Why do that, just because of an unimportant argument over clothes?'

Sara supposed he had a point. It was very galling to have to admit it, though. And she still didn't like the high-handed way he had gone about this.

'Where are these clothes you've bought for me?' she said at last, in a voice that was still slightly resentful.

He left the kitchen, and came back a minute later with a couple of large bags.

'Here,' he said, tossing them over to her with a smile. 'I had to guess the sizes, but I'm pretty good at that sort of thing,' he finished, with a lazily appreciative look at the curves of her body.

Sara half turned away, so that he wouldn't see that his gaze had made her suddenly feel rather hot. To hide her unexpected confusion, she tipped the bags out on to the kitchen-table. Then her nose wrinkled daintily as she saw what he had bought.

'Jeans?' she said, holding up a couple of pairs of denims.

'Comfortable and practical,' Lucas told her. His gaze drifted downwards. 'And you've got a gorgeous bottom,' he went on a little more huskily. 'You'll look really good in them.'

Sara ignored that remark. Instead, she sorted through the bright sweatshirts that she was evidently meant to wear with the jeans. Then she picked up the last items he had bought. 'Gym shoes?' she said, raising her eyebrows.

'Trainers. You'll be able to walk around in them all day, and not get aching feet.'

'I'm surprised you didn't get me a hat, as well,' she retorted. 'One just like yours!'

'Mine's a one-off,' he said cheerfully. 'Although I could probably get you one very like it, if you really want one.'

'No, thanks,' she said with some feeling. Then she looked at the clothes again. 'I never wear these sort of things,' she said at last.

'I guessed you didn't. But why don't you give them a try?'

'If I don't like them, will you give me my own clothes back again?'

He shrugged. 'I suppose I'll have to. I can't let you walk around half-naked—although, personally, I wouldn't have any objections,' he added, his eyes suddenly gleaming in that disturbing way they had of doing. 'Incidentally, I decided to let you keep your underwear.'

'How very good of you!'

'My pleasure,' he said easily. 'Although, to be perfectly honest, I shouldn't think that Edward finds it very exciting. If you want my advice, try some silk and lace in the future. Cotton's very practical, but it's a bit of a passion-killer.'

'When I want your advice about my underwear, I'll ask for it! I'm sure you're quite an authority on the subject,' she added, with deliberate sarcasm.

'I've had some experience in these matters,' Lucas confirmed modestly.

Sara gave a loud snort, grabbed hold of the clothes, and then flounced out of the kitchen. She couldn't cope with this sort of conversation this early in the morning.

Back in her own room again, she wriggled into the jeans, pulled on one of the sweatshirts, and then laced up the trainers. Then she stood back and looked at her reflection in the full-length mirror.

She hardly recognised herself. The girl who stared back at her looked a couple of years younger, and unexpectedly carefree. And when she twisted round for a back view, she realised something else. Lucas had been right. Her rear end definitely looked good in tight-fitting denim!

She studied herself one last time; then she gave a faint sigh. How Edward would hate it if he could see her now. These were precisely the kind of clothes that he didn't like her to wear. He approved of fairly formal dress at all times. Perhaps she should just enjoy being able to wear this sort of stuff for the next couple of days. Once she got back to England she would have to dump it, and go back to the suits and blouses that Edward approved of.

Since she could hardly wear her hair scraped back into its usual rather severe style, she just clipped it back at the temples and left the rest of it to fall in a dark swirl over her shoulders. Worn like this, it made her green eyes seem even larger, and somehow more mysterious.

Sara gave another small sigh as she finally turned away from the mirror. She had better not get used to looking like this. This was only a very temporary phase in her life, and she had to keep on remembering that.

As she walked slowly back into the kitchen, she felt unexpectedly self-conscious. Lucas turned round to look at her, and his gaze very clearly told her that he liked what he saw.

'Much better,' he said softly, at last. 'You finally look as if you belong to the twentieth century.'

Sara lifted her head. 'I'm sure that I looked fine before.'

'Yes, you did,' he agreed equably. 'You'd look good in whatever you wore. But right now you're an absolute knock-out.'

'Just because I'm wearing jeans and a sweatshirt?' she said in some disbelief.

'It's not only that. You've finally let your hair down—quite literally,' he finished with a grin. 'You're more relaxed. You've started to let go.'

'I'm only wearing these things for a couple of days,' she warned. 'Once the sightseeing's over, I'll be back in my own clothes again.'

Lucas didn't seem worried. 'Perhaps after a couple of days, you'll like your new look so much that you'll want to keep it,' he suggested.

'I can't do that.'

His eyes narrowed a fraction. 'Why not?' he asked, in a tone that had suddenly become noticeably cooler. 'Because Edward wouldn't like it?'

'That's right.'

'And are you going to let Edward's likes and dislikes rule the rest of your life?'

'He's my fiancé. I want to please him,' she said, her tone suddenly stiff.

Lucas growled something under his breath, and certainly didn't seem pleased by her reply. Then he strode towards the door.

'We'd better leave now,' he said briefly. 'The train goes at seven.'

A taxi was waiting outside to take them to the railway station. Lucas bundled her into it, gave the driver quick instructions in Spanish, and then settled himself in beside her.

For some reason, Sara felt more conscious than usual of Lucas's nearness. Perhaps it was the clothes she was wearing, she told herself a little uneasily. They made her feel—different.

Or perhaps it was those kisses he had given her yesterday, murmured a soft voice inside her head.

'No!' she said. Then, realising that she had actually spoken out loud and that Lucas was looking at her quizzically, she flushed. 'I was—er—thinking of something,' she said rather lamely.

Lucas merely raised one eyebrow, and didn't ask any awkward questions, which was a great relief to Sara.

When they reached the station, they found it was already crowded.

'Are all these people going to Machu Picchu?' she asked in surprise.

'I told you, it's one of Peru's major tourist attractions. Forget about your manners and let's shove to the front,' Lucas advised. 'Or we might not get a seat.'

When the train arrived, Lucas caught hold of Sara's hand and hauled her aboard with all the speed and agility of the experienced traveller. He quickly found seats for them, and Sara flopped down slightly breathlessly. Then she realised that Lucas was still holding her hand.

'You can let go of me now,' she said, a trifle awkwardly.

His long fingers moved over the back of her hand, while his thumb gently caressed her palm. Tiny shivers ran up her arm, and she knew he was aware of them. For just a moment, he looked pleased. Then he removed his hand, and Sara released her pent-up breath.

'How long will it take to get there?' she asked, aware that she was gabbling slightly.

'Four hours. And that's provided there aren't any hold-ups or breakdowns,' he added.

'Four hours?' she squeaked. 'I didn't know it was going to take that long!'

'Just sit back and enjoy the journey,' he advised, relaxing back into his own seat.

There wasn't much else Sara could do. The train finally zigzagged its way out of Cuzco on a steep climb, and then the track began to drop its way gently through mainly agricultural country.

'Do you want something to eat?' Lucas asked after a while. 'Teresa left us a packed lunch.'

'What's on offer?'

'I've no idea.' He investigated the neatly wrapped parcels. 'Cold chicken, sandwiches and fresh fruit,' he announced at last. 'No Peruvian delicacies, I'm afraid. Perhaps that's just as well, though. One of the traditional dishes of this part of the Andes is roast guinea pig.'

Sara turned faintly green. 'I think I just lost my appetite.'

Lucas grinned. 'Try a sandwich. And don't worry,' he added, his eyes glittering mischievously. 'There's nothing more alarming than cheese in them.'

The train rattled on for what seemed, to Sara, to be a very long time. When it finally began to draw to a halt, she perked up a little. 'Is this it?' she asked hopefully.

'Not yet. This is Ollantaytambo. But the scenery gets a lot more spectacular from here on.'

He was right. Ahead was a wide sunlit gorge, with high mountains beyond. A turbulent river coursed its way through the gorge, and they had marvellous views from the train.

'We should be there fairly soon,' Lucas told her some time later. 'There'll be buses waiting to take us from the station to Machu Picchu itself.'

Sara groaned at the thought of yet more travelling. She just hoped that Machu Picchu would turn out to be worth it.

After they finally got off the train, Lucas found them a couple of seats right at the front of one of the buses which, a few minutes later, began to wheeze its way up a steep, zigzagging road. Sara was beginning to wonder if they were ever going to reach the ruins. They were certainly hard enough to get to!

'No wonder everyone calls it the *lost* city of the Incas,' she grumbled to Lucas. 'In fact, it was a miracle that it was ever found in the first place!'

'An American historian called Hiram Bingham almost literally stumbled across it, nearly eighty years ago. He thought it was the lost city he had been searching for, and so he was the one who gave it that tag. A lot more research has been done since then, though, and the general theory now is that Machu Picchu was never "lost" at all. It was just abandoned by the Incas at some time in the past, for reasons that we'll probably never know about.'

'Why did they live in such a way-out place?' she asked curiously. 'It's in the middle of nowhere!'

'It probably wasn't a "city" at all,' explained Lucas. 'All the signs indicate that it was some sort of cere- monial centre.' A smile touched the corners of his mouth. 'When they excavated the site, a lot more female skeletons were found than male. One theory was that these were Sun Virgins, who catered to the needs of the male Incas. Rather a nice idea, don't you think?' he murmured thoughtfully.

'No, I don't!' Sara replied with some indignation.

He grinned. 'It's a theory that's generally dis- counted now, anyway. When it comes down to it, Machu Picchu is a mystery—and perhaps that's the way it should remain.'

The bus finally jerked to a halt, and all the pas- sengers piled off. Sara was about to follow the rest of the crowd, but Lucas caught hold of her arm. 'Let them go ahead and spread themselves out,' he ad- vised. 'We'll have something to eat first.'

He seated himself, cross-legged, on a nearby patch of grass. Then he began to open the packages of food that they had saved for their lunch.

Sara seated herself beside him, wriggling around a little as she tried to get comfortable on the rather hard ground. She was more used to eating in discreetly expensive restaurants with Edward.

Lucas shared out the food, then he settled back and began to eat.

'You always look relaxed,' Sara observed. 'And you never seem to be in any great hurry to get anywhere. Don't you ever get uptight, like other people?'

'Of course I do. But there's something about this country that encourages you to take things at an easy pace,' he replied. 'Even you're a lot less strung up than when I first saw you.'

Sara wasn't at all sure that she agreed with him over that. There were times when she was around Lucas Farraday when she was *very* strung up indeed!

She ate slowly, not really thinking about the food, but instead reflecting on how very different the last few days had been, compared to what she had expected. Instead of a short trip to Peru and a heated showdown with Clarissa, she had travelled all these miles with a complete stranger. And it looked as if she would be spending yet more time in his company, because he was certainly showing no signs of wanting to move on.

Not that he was really a stranger any more, she admitted to herself with a wry grimace. She supposed it was because they had spent so many hours together—and often in very close proximity. In fact, it was slightly alarming how used she was getting to having him around.

Sara looked up to find that Lucas had stopped eating, and was instead studying her very closely. She always found it a little unnerving when his dark blue gaze took on that intense sort of look. She much preferred it when his gaze was light, and he looked faintly amused. It was definitely a lot less disturbing.

'Lost your appetite?' she enquired slightly edgily, as he made no effort to touch the rest of his food.

'For some things,' he said slowly.

Sara wasn't sure how to take that remark. In the end, she decided to ignore it. That didn't seem to please Lucas, though. And his gaze never left her face.

Sara shifted uneasily. 'Your mood's changed a bit, hasn't it?'

'When I'm around you, my mood changes quite frequently,' he told her softly. 'It's just that you don't notice it most of the time.'

For some reason, that rather nettled her. 'You mean I'm unobservant?'

'Or perhaps you just don't care enough to take any notice of the way I'm feeling—or what I want,' Lucas finished, his gaze suddenly fixing on her again with vivid intentness.

Sara decided that this was all suddenly getting far too personal.

'I'm not in the mood for this sort of conversation,' she said briskly, jumping to her feet. 'Anyway, I think we should move on. Let's take a look at this lost city.'

Lucas didn't get up straight away, though. 'Is this what you usually do when you're confronted with something you don't know how to deal with? Just walk away from it?'

'I'm not walking away from anything,' she denied, just a little too vehemently. 'But we've just spent four bone-aching hours on that train getting here. I think we ought to take a look at Machu Picchu before it's time to go back again!'

Much to her surprise—and relief—Lucas didn't say another word. He gathered together the remains of their lunch, then he silently stood up and began to walk towards the ticket gate.

Sara frowned lightly. She had never seen him quite like this before. In the end, though, she gave a small shrug and began to walk after him. She supposed everyone had a slightly darker side to their character. Lucas couldn't be expected to be relaxed and easy-going *all* the time.

A footpath finally brought them to the actual ruins of Machu Picchu. Long stepped terraces stretched out in front of them with, beyond that, the ruins of temples and palaces, all laid out against the soaring backdrop of the surrounding mountains. Sara just stood and stared for quite a long while. She had to admit the long trip had been worth it, to see a site like this. The setting was magnificent, and the atmosphere just a little eerie, as if an ancient Inca might, without any warning, materialise right in front of her.

They wandered past the terraces and then, instead of heading into the main section of the ruins, Lucas led her up a long stone staircase that climbed up fairly steeply.

'Where are we going?' panted Sara a couple of minutes later, already out of breath.

'Wait and see,' he replied, a little mysteriously.

The steps eventually ended at a spur of rock. Sara finally got her breath back. Then she lifted her head and let her gaze roam over the view that was stretched out in front of her.

'It's fantastic,' she murmured at last.

'Worth the climb?' enquired Lucas, gently raising one dark blond eyebrow.

'Yes!' She stared for ages at the ruins that were spread out below her. Machu Picchu—the lost city—was set on a plateau in the centre of soaring mountains, topped with wraiths of cloud. The sun had broken through, shining down on the pattern of broken walls that marked the remains of what had once been impressive buildings, and Sara had to admit that the whole scene was quite awesome.

'I wish I had a camera,' she said regretfully.

'Just keep the picture in your memory,' advised Lucas quietly. 'That way, it'll never fade or get lost.'

She turned towards him. Then she found that he was looking at *her*, instead of at the magnificent view in front of him. And something about his brilliant blue gaze made her feel unexpectedly weak around the knees.

'I'm glad that you m-made me come here,' she babbled, her tongue tripping slightly over the words as a fresh wave of nervousness swept over her. 'I mean, I know I wasn't keen on the idea, but I really wouldn't have wanted to have missed this.'

'Perhaps I can talk you into one or two other things, as well,' Lucas suggested softly.

'More sightseeing trips?' said Sara, quite deliberately misunderstanding him. 'Thanks, but I really don't think there'll be time. I'll probably be meeting up with my stepmother soon after we get back...'

Something about the look on his face made her voice trail away. Edgily, she glanced around, and realised that there were no other people nearby. They were all down at the main site, scrambling around the ruins. She and Lucas were alone up here, far above the crowds of tourists. Sara nibbled the bottom of her lip rather uncertainly.

'I—er—I think I've seen enough of this view,' she said in a voice that, to her consternation, still had a noticeable quaver in it. 'Let's go down and take a look at the main ruins.'

'If that's what you want,' Lucas agreed at once.

Since she had been expecting all this to end in a rather awkward—and perhaps even embarrassing— tussle, she was so surprised that, for a few moments, she didn't even move. Then she rather hurriedly began to walk towards the steps. She supposed she ought to escape while she still had the chance!

At the last moment, though, Lucas fell into step beside her and smoothly slid his hand through her own.

'Just in case you lose your footing,' he said in a relaxed voice.

'I didn't stumble on the way up,' she pointed out, trying to withdraw her hand from his, but finding it much harder than she had expected to free her fingers from his light grip.

'No, you didn't,' Lucas agreed affably. 'But going down is always more difficult. And I wouldn't want anything to happen to you,' he finished, his eyes taking on a distinct gleam.

Sara decided that it really wasn't worth arguing with him. Once they were back in the main part of the ruins, he would *have* to let go of her again. There would be other people around by then. If he still wouldn't release her, then she only had to yell for help. Someone was sure to come to her aid.

Then it suddenly struck her as perfectly ridiculous that she should need help in getting away from Lucas. After all, he could hardly be described as dangerous!

In fact, if she really wanted to be rid of him, then she only had to tell him very firmly to leave her alone.

Only she seemed to have tried that several times already, and it didn't appear to have worked. Perhaps because you didn't really say it with any conviction? argued a small voice inside her head.

Sara immediately stiffened her shoulders. Of *course* she had meant it! It was just that this man was too thick-skinned to get the message.

She quickened her pace, almost taking the steps at a bound. Lucas easily kept up with her, though. And he didn't loosen his grip on her hand.

His fingers were warm and firm around her own. It was rather alarming how she was beginning to enjoy that pleasant physical contact between them.

You're in a strange country, she argued with herself. It's bound to make you feel better if you're with someone who's familiar.

Then she sighed. One moment, she was telling herself that she only wanted to get away from Lucas. The next, she was completely contradicting herself. She really was getting awfully confused.

As if sensing her mood, Lucas came to a sudden halt. They were only yards away from the bottom of the steps, but still out of sight of everyone else exploring the ruins.

'It's no good,' he murmured. 'There are some temptations that you just have to give in to.'

Before she had a chance to ask him what he meant, he closed his mouth over hers and took a quick but unexpectedly fierce kiss from her.

Sara was caught off balance, and didn't have a chance to put up any resistance. She felt his tongue slide briefly into the sweetness of her mouth, but before she had time to gasp in surprise—Edward *never* did anything like that—he had withdrawn again, and she was left with an entirely unexpected sensation of regret that he hadn't explored further. The kiss didn't end there, though. His lips moved over hers in a warm caress, the fierceness gone now, leaving only a gentle pleasure in its wake.

Sara felt unexpectedly dizzy by the time he finally released her. Then she slowly began to remember that she had no business kissing this man. She belonged to someone else.

'That really wasn't necessary,' she told him in a stiff voice.

'I'm afraid that it was *very* necessary—at least, from my point of view,' came Lucas's dry reply. 'And I did enjoy it,' he went on in a much more husky tone. 'In fact, I'd rather like to repeat it.'

'Well, you can't,' she said rather too shrilly. 'You'll just have to find someone else if you're that desperate for some woman to kiss.'

'But I don't want just any woman,' Lucas told her with disconcerting directness. 'I want you.'

'You can't have me!' Sara could hear a slightly desperate note in her voice, and that frightened her. What on earth was happening to her? She hardly ever lost control like this. 'You can't!' she repeated with fresh vehemence.

Lucas gave a small shrug of acceptance, and then turned away from her. Disappointment instantly flooded right through her. Was he just going to give up? Hadn't he meant what he had said?

Then she was immediately horrified by her own reaction. Oh, this was getting ridiculous, she told herself shakily. She was reaching the point where she didn't even seem to know her own mind!

She had the feeling that Lucas knew it, though—
that he had only turned away because he had decided
the time wasn't quite right.

And what would happen when he decided the time
was right? Sara gave a small shiver. She didn't even
want to think about that. She just had to keep on
thinking about Edward; imagine that his ring was still
on her finger, instead of sitting in his safe, back in
England.

Only she was a little terrified to discover that she
couldn't seem to remember exactly what Edward
looked like. Whenever she tried to picture his face,
the image that floated in front of her was blurred and
indistinct. If only she had a photo of him——

Then she gave herself a mental shake. She didn't
need a photo of her fiancé to remember what he
looked like! she told herself with new resolution. This
preoccupation with Lucas Farraday wouldn't last.

She repeated that to herself silently one more time,
to make sure it was fixed inside her head. Then she
firmly turned her back on Lucas, and marched down
to the ruins.

CHAPTER SIX

SARA and Lucas spent the next couple of hours exploring the ruins of Machu Picchu. Sara felt safe among the crowds of tourists, and made sure that she didn't move too far away from them. Lucas looked a little moody, though, and frowned as they nearly bumped into yet another large group of people.

'This is no way to see a place like this,' he growled. 'There are far too many people around.'

In the middle of the afternoon, though, the crowds suddenly began to thin out. Sara didn't take very much notice at first. She was exploring the far end of the ruins, and wondering if she had the energy to climb to the top of the cliff above Machu Picchu. There was a well-maintained trail, and the views would be incredible, she thought. She had been told the walk would take about an hour, though, and she regretfully decided there really wasn't time. They would have to be heading back to Cuzco fairly soon.

By the time she wandered back to the main part of the ruins, there were even less people around. Sara looked around rather uneasily. Where had everyone gone? Then she glanced at her watch. A moment later, her eyebrows shot up. She hadn't realised how late it was getting.

She hurried over to Lucas. 'We'd better start heading back to the buses. If we don't get back to the station fairly soon we'll miss the train.'

'We've already missed it,' he told her calmly.

Sara blinked in disbelief. 'But—we can't have! How will we get back to Cuzco?'

'We won't—not until tomorrow,' replied Lucas, in the same unperturbed voice. 'But there's a hotel just outside the ruins that caters for tourists who want to stay overnight. With luck, we'll be able to get a couple of rooms.'

'You planned all this without even asking me?' she said incredulously.

'If I'd asked you, you'd have said no. You always do. Although I'm not sure that you always mean it,' he added thoughtfully.

'Well, I'd certainly have meant it this time! I don't *want* to stay overnight.'

'You didn't want to come to Machu Picchu,' he reminded her. 'But you liked it once you got here. And you don't actually have much choice about staying. We can't get back to Cuzco until tomorrow.'

The high-handedness of this man infuriated Sara. He was at it again, trying to organise her life for her. No, not just *trying*—he was actually doing it! If only there were some way of getting out of here under her own steam. She would have hitched a lift on a llama, if only it were possible! Unfortunately, she was forced to admit that wasn't a very practical plan. In fact, once she had begun to calm down a little, she realised that Lucas had once again got his own way. She was stuck here for the night. She didn't like it, but there wasn't anything she could actually *do* about it.

Except make him pay, of course—quite literally.

'Well, I hope you've got plenty of cash on you,' she said to him coolly. 'If you're going to make me stay in some hotel in the middle of nowhere, then you can pick up the bill. And you might as well know right now that I want a decent room, and it's got to have a bath with lashings of hot water. On top of that, I expect a decent dinner. Oh, and you're going to have to buy me some nightwear. I didn't bring any with me, since I didn't know you were going to force me to stay here.'

'When I'm in a situation like this, I usually sleep in just my underpants,' Lucas remarked.

'I prefer a more conventional sort of nightwear,' Sara replied at once, pointedly ignoring his hint.

Lucas suddenly grinned. 'Pyjamas that button right up to the neck?'

The accuracy of his guess got her annoyed all over again.

'I don't see anything wrong with pyjamas! Anyway, how did you know——?' She suddenly stopped, not at all sure that she wanted him to answer that question.

Lucas only grinned even more broadly, though. 'A girl who wears sensible cotton underwear is almost sure to wear pyjamas. It looks as if it's not only your ordinary clothes that need updating. Your undies and nightwear need a change of image. I think I'm going to have to teach you how to be adventurous in all sorts of different ways,' he finished thoughtfully, his gaze suddenly alight.

'I'm not the adventurous sort,' Sara retorted. 'And I don't *want* to change.'

Lucas stopped smiling. 'Oh, I think that you do,' he said in a very different tone of voice. 'It's just that you won't admit it yet.'

Sara decided to ignore him. That was the only thing to do when his voice took on that throaty note and he looked at her in that particular way.

She set off towards the hotel, and just hoped that they had a couple of vacancies. If not, it certainly wasn't going to improve her temper!

She waited in the reception area while Lucas went to fix up their rooms. He was such a long time that she began to suspect he was having some difficulty. He finally came back with a pleased look on his face, though.

'Well?' she demanded. 'Did you get the rooms?'

'We were lucky. There was a last-minute cancellation.'

'You mean, *you* were lucky,' Sara told him darkly. 'If the hotel had been fully booked, you'd have been in real trouble. I'm not the type who likes sleeping rough. Has my room got a bath?'

'It's got a bath,' he confirmed.

'Good. Then I think I'll go up and have a hot soak.'

Lucas glanced casually at his watch. 'It's getting late. Perhaps we'd better have dinner first.'

'I can't go in looking like this,' she objected.

His gaze ran over her appraisingly. 'You look fine,' he said at last. 'And no one expects you to dress up. They're used to serving dinner to people who've spent the day tramping over the ruins.' Before she had a chance to argue further, he firmly shepherded her towards the dining-room.

'I'm going to choose the most expensive dishes on the menu,' Sara warned, as they sat down at one of the tables. 'It's no more than you deserve, after the way you've behaved today!'

Lucas didn't seem in the least concerned. 'Have whatever you like,' he offered generously. 'And as for my behaviour,' he went on thoughtfully, 'I don't remember doing anything too terrible. I did kiss you, of course,' he recalled, his words bringing a distinct blush to her face. 'But I didn't think you minded that too much. In fact, I got the clear impression that you rather liked it. And now I'm buying you a very expensive dinner at a very expensive hotel. Not many girls would object to that.'

'Is it *too* expensive?' Sara queried, a slightly worried frown wrinkling her forehead. She forgot about her intentions of making him pay dearly for the trick he had played on her. 'I mean——' She tried to think of a tactful way of phrasing her question. 'Well—are you sure you can afford it?' she finally blurted out.

'They haven't cancelled my credit cards yet,' Lucas said drily. Then, seeing the real concern on her face, his own features altered. 'Don't worry,' he said with an unexpectedly gentle smile. 'I can afford it.'

Sara was starving. She had had nothing to eat all day except the packed lunch that Teresa had prepared for them. She worked her way through the menu and, an hour later, finally sat back with a contented smile on her face.

'That's better,' she said. 'Right now, I'm in such a good mood that I'm almost prepared to like you.'

'Then perhaps I'd better feed you up more often,' Lucas commented. 'It's not often that you admit to liking me! In fact, I don't recall it ever happening before.' His mouth twitched at the corners. 'Perhaps I ought to take advantage of it before you change your mind.'

Sara found herself watching his mouth with unexpected fascination. It was such a nice shape. And very expressive, when he wanted it to be. Sometimes, she could guess his mood from just the line of his lips.

Then, realising that she was beginning to show far too much interest in him, she hurriedly looked away from him.

'I don't *mind* it when you look at me,' Lucas said softly. 'In fact, I rather like it.'

'I wasn't looking at you!' she denied instantly. 'I was just ... just ...' Her voice ran out as she realised that she couldn't actually come up with any plausible excuse for her sudden interest in him.

Lucas's eyes narrowed slightly, and he seemed about to say something. At the last moment, though, he apparently changed his mind and instead got to his feet.

'Do you want something to drink?' he asked. 'The bar's still open.'

'No, thanks. I think I'll turn in. I'm rather tired.'

Sara had decided that she needed to get away from Lucas for a while. Whenever she spent too much time with him, he started to get to her in a rather odd way. She found herself staring at him, noticing his good points instead of his faults, and not really minding too much when he casually touched her—as he seemed to do quite often.

Lucas walked up the stairs with her, so she supposed he had decided to have an early night, as well. He led her to a room on the first floor, unlocked the door with a key which he produced from his pocket, and then stood back a fraction.

'This is it,' he told her.

'Thanks. I'll see you in the morning.'

As she walked through the doorway, though, Lucas followed her inside.

Sara turned round and glared at him, her good mood rather rapidly beginning to dissipate.

'You don't seem to be getting the message. I've already said goodnight to you!'

'I know,' Lucas agreed equably. 'But there's something I didn't tell you earlier. The hotel only had one cancellation. We're going to have to share this room.'

Sara's nerves immediately twitched. 'We certainly are not!' she shot back at once.

Lucas had already closed the door behind him, though, and she could see it was going to be very difficult to lever him out of here. That didn't mean she was going to give up, though. There was no way she was going to spend the night with him!

'There's no need to get so uptight about this,' commented Lucas, seeing the look on her face. 'I haven't said that I intend to sleep with you—although that doesn't mean I don't want to,' he added, his eyes darkening several shades. 'I've simply said that we'll have to share this room for tonight. Don't make a big issue out of it, Sara. There's plenty of space for the two of us to spread ourselves around. We don't even have to come within touching distance of each other— if we don't want to,' he added in a faintly mocking tone.

Sara flushed, both at the bluntness of his words, and because he was making her feel as if she were behaving very childishly. That didn't change anything, though. She didn't want to spend the next few hours so very close to him.

'You'll just have to make other arrangements,' she said in a rather tense voice. 'There must be another room you can use. Perhaps they'll put up a makeshift bed for you somewhere——'

'I'm sleeping here,' Lucas told her, calmly but firmly. 'You've already got used to having me around during the day. Well, I think it's about time you got used to me being around at night.'

But that didn't seem at all like a good idea to Sara. 'I don't see the point of it,' she insisted. 'Why should I get used to having you around?'

His blue gaze rested on her placidly. 'Haven't you worked it out yet? We're going to spend the rest of our lives together, Sara. So we might as well start getting to know each other even better than we do right now.'

With that, he disappeared into the shower. And by the time she had finally found her voice again the water was running, and there was no point in flinging her slightly frantic questions at him.

Sara slumped down on the edge of the bed. This was definitely getting completely out of hand! How could they possibly spend the rest of their lives together? She was going to marry *Edward*. Lucas knew that—she had made it perfectly clear to him—so why was he keeping up this silly, pointless charade?

By the time he finally emerged from the shower, Sara had managed to collect herself together and was feeling more in control of herself. She had already worked out what she was going to say. He had to understand that this had to come to a *stop*. A joke was all very well, but he was beginning to carry it much too far.

The sight of Lucas ambling into the room with just a towel tied casually around his waist, though, sent all her carefully worked-out speech spinning right out of her head. His shaggy dark blond hair was damp and clinging to his head in an untidy cluster of curls, his skin gleamed with the moisture that still clung to it, and he seemed to have chosen a very *small* towel. It covered just the necessities, and left her with an excellent view of his powerfully muscled legs.

Sara found herself swallowing rather hard. She had to admit that this man was very well put together.

'What you said earlier—about the two of us spending the rest of our lives together,' she said in a slightly croaky voice. 'You do know, of course, that it's quite impossible?'

'I don't know any such thing,' Lucas replied calmly. 'All things are possible—especially if you're prepared to make things happen.'

Sara didn't like the sound of that. It made her feel as if she was beginning to lose control over her own life.

'It *is* impossible,' she insisted stiffly. 'You've known that right from the very beginning.'

'Because of Edward? But he isn't here at the moment—and I am,' Lucas reminded her gently.

'That doesn't mean——' Sara began. Then her eyes suddenly flew wide open. 'What are you doing?' she demanded.

Lucas stopped unwinding the towel. 'Sorry,' he grinned. 'I suppose I should have warned you. I'm about to put on a clean pair of underpants.'

'Couldn't you have done that in the bathroom?' she said in a freezing tone.

He gave a relaxed shrug. 'I suppose I could have. I don't want to keep any secrets from you, though, Sara. And it certainly doesn't embarrass me to be around you like this.'

'And what if it embarrasses *me*?' came Sara's slightly shrill reply.

'Why should it? We come in different shapes and sizes, but we're all built from the same basic model. There's nothing embarrassing about a body.'

His matter-of-fact tone actually made her relax a fraction. It also made her feel as if she was being ridiculously prudish. And perhaps she was, she told herself with a small sigh. Maybe she was even overreacting about sharing a room with him. After all, they had already spent hours wedged together on buses and trains. Was there any difference in sleeping in the same room? Especially when there would be a safe distance between them? Then her head shot up suspiciously. But what if there wasn't a safe distance between them? What if he was planning on there being no distance at all?

'Where are you intending to sleep?' she demanded bluntly.

Lucas's gaze rested on the double bed. 'It should take two people quite easily,' he suggested. Then his eyes shone with amusement. 'We could build a barricade of pillows down the middle, if you want to feel really safe.'

'No,' she said at once.

His eyes gleamed hopefully. 'To the barricade of pillows?'

'To the bed! I'm not sharing it with you.'

'I rather thought that you wouldn't,' Lucas murmured, and she could hear the clear regret in his voice. 'Well, that leaves one other choice.' He glanced over at the chair that stood on the far side of the room. 'I suppose one of us could sleep quite comfortably in that. I'll toss you for it.'

Sara was immediately outraged. 'Toss me for it? If you were a gentleman, you wouldn't even suggest such a thing!'

'I am a gentleman—most of the time. But I also like a good night's sleep. If you won't share the bed with me, then I think the least you can do is take your chances with the chair.' He fished a coin out of his pocket. 'Heads or tails?' he enquired.

Sara decided to stick to a dignified silence.

'Opting out?' enquired Lucas. 'That's OK by me. I'll toss *and* call.' He flipped the coin into the air. 'Heads,' he guessed, as the coin spun over and over. Then he neatly caught it, and turned it on to the back of his hand. 'Heads it is,' he said, as he looked at it.

Then he gave Sara a sly grin. 'It looks as if this is my lucky day.'

With a tremendous effort, Sara managed to hold her tongue. If she did say anything, she knew it would only be something *very* rude.

'Since the choice is mine, I'll take the bed,' Lucas decided. He shot another of those infuriating grins at Sara. 'Of course, you're welcome to share it with me. And I promise not to lay a finger on you—unless it's by request.'

'I don't want you to touch me, and I don't want to share a bed with you,' Sara told him coldly. With that, she lifted her head very high into the air, and marched into the bathroom.

Once inside, she finally let go and practically gibbered with rage. The man had *deliberately* booked a double room—*deliberately* tried to make her share a bed with him! Well, it wasn't going to work. She would sleep on the floor rather than let him get away with this.

A long, hot shower finally helped her to think more clearly. And once she had calmed down a little the obvious solution occurred to her. All she had to do was phone down to the reception desk and ask to be given another room.

She finished showering, hurriedly dried herself, and was then faced with the problem of what to wear. She had already rinsed out her undies, and they were now hanging wetly over the towel rail.

In the end, she grabbed the biggest towel she could find—which was *much* larger than the one Lucas had used—wound it tightly around herself, and then marched back into the bedroom.

Lucas was already sprawled out on the bed, and looked half asleep. She wasn't fooled by those half-closed eyes, though. She was ready to bet that he was far more alert than he gave the impression of being.

She went over to the phone, picked up the receiver, and asked for the reception desk.

'No use asking for another room, sweetheart,' murmured Lucas. 'There aren't any.'

It always annoyed her when he read her mind so easily. Sara rather pointedly turned her back on him, and gave a sigh of relief when a voice answered at the other end of the phone.

'Oh—hello,' she said. 'I'm sorry to bother you, but my room isn't—isn't suitable. Could I possibly change to another one?'

The voice at the other end was very polite and very apologetic. He was extremely sorry, but the hotel was fully booked. There wasn't a vacant room in the entire place. What exactly was wrong with the room? Was it something that he, personally, could put right for her?

Yes, you can come and remove this man from my bed! she wanted to yell at him. Instead, she somehow choked back the words and told him that it was all right, she would stay where she was.

As she put down the receiver, she turned and glared at Lucas. 'I hope you don't get a wink of sleep in that damned bed!'

'I can usually sleep just about anywhere,' he replied in an unperturbed voice. Then he looked at her thoughtfully. 'And talking of sleep—are you going to wear that towel all night? It won't be very comfortable.'

'There isn't much alternative,' she reminded him furiously. 'I wasn't planning on spending the night here!'

'You're getting uptight again,' he observed. 'There's no need to be, you know. I'm not going to wait until the light's turned out, and then pounce on you.'

'You'd better not,' she warned. 'You might be a lot bigger and stronger than me, but I can yell loudly enough, if I need to. I'd raise the entire hotel in seconds!'

Lucas's eyes brightened. 'You might find that you don't *want* to raise the hotel. You certainly didn't mind when I kissed you this afternoon,' he reminded her with a glint of mischief.

'I wasn't given any *chance* to object,' she muttered, suddenly finding herself thrown on to the defensive.

'Weren't you?' he mused. 'I was under the impression that I gave you plenty of time. But don't let's argue about it now. We were trying to settle the question of what you can wear to bed. How about a T-shirt?' he suggested, sliding off the bed and sorting through his rucksack. 'I always carry a clean spare.'

He chucked a large, baggy T-shirt over to her, and Sara didn't have much option except to catch it. She was just about to tell him that she had no intention of wearing it, when common sense took over. She didn't actually have much choice. After all, there wasn't anything else. And it *was* only a T-shirt.

She went back into the bathroom, ditched the towel and wriggled into the T-shirt. It fell to mid-thigh, and felt soft and comfortable. As she went back into the bedroom, though, she felt absurdly self-conscious.

Lucas's gaze slid over her with approval. 'Very nice,' he commented. 'And *very* sexy.'

'It's just a T-shirt,' she snapped at him, for some reason feeling horribly edgy again. Really, when she was with this man, her moods seem to swing wildly from one extreme to the other. That was something that didn't usually happen to her, and she didn't like it.

'Going to risk the bed?' Lucas enquired with some interest. 'That chair doesn't look very comfortable.'

'I'm sure it will be fine.' She grabbed a blanket from the bed, marched over to the chair, and settled herself down into it. It was even harder than it looked, and she knew at once that she wasn't going to get much sleep.

'If you just trusted me, you'd have a much more restful night,' Lucas pointed out.

'I'm perfectly all right,' Sara lied. 'Please turn out the light. I'm going to sleep now.'

Only she didn't go to sleep, of course. She decided that not even a contortionist could have slept in that chair. She wriggled around silently, determined that Lucas wouldn't hear her restless movements and know just how uncomfortable she was. No matter which way she lay, though, some part of the chair dug into her, or else her muscles started to cramp. After a couple of hours, she finally sat up and let out an exasperated sigh.

In the near-darkness, she could just make out the shape of the bed. Lucas's body was no more than a pale blur, but she was sure he hadn't moved at all. He was obviously getting a very good night's sleep.

'Rat!' she muttered under her breath. Edward would never have done anything like this, leaving her to spend the night in a chair. Edward was a gentleman!

And just a little dull? murmured a traitorous voice inside her head. Would Edward have dragged you off to see the lost city of the Incas? Teased and kissed you? Shared a room with you?

A little panic-stricken, Sara put a sharp brake on her wandering thoughts. She liked Edward exactly the way he was. After all, she was going to marry him, wasn't she?

She decided she was only thinking these odd thoughts because she was extremely tired, and needed sleep. But she definitely wasn't going to get it in this chair.

Sara looked longingly towards the bed. Perhaps she could lie on the very edge of the mattress? That way, there would be absolutely no contact between her and Lucas. In fact, he must be very soundly asleep by now. He wouldn't even know she was there. And she could creep back to the chair before he woke up in the morning.

She stared indecisively at the bed for several more minutes. Then, with a sudden surge of determination, she got up and tiptoed towards it.

As she stood beside it, Lucas didn't stir. He was obviously deeply asleep. Provided she moved silently and carefully, she could just slide in the other side, and he wouldn't know a thing about it.

She sidled round to the far side of the bed and pulled back the sheet. The thumping of her heart seemed horribly loud, and she had to remind herself that no one but her could hear it. Anyway, what was there to be scared of? She was getting into a bed, that was all.

Sara sat gingerly on the edge, and waited for a few more moments. When there was still no sound or movement from Lucas, she gave a small sigh of relief and slid under the sheet.

The softness of the mattress felt like pure bliss after that chair. Her eyes were really heavy by now, and she thankfully closed them. It wasn't going to take her more than a couple of minutes to fall asleep.

'I wondered how long you were going to stick it out in that chair,' commented Lucas's voice in the darkness. 'I thought you'd creep over long before this.'

Sara's eyes flew wide open again. 'Why aren't you asleep?' she demanded.

'I don't think I'm ever going to sleep very much while you're around,' Lucas replied huskily.

Sara started to scramble into a sitting position, but Lucas laid a restraining hand on her arm.

'There's no need to panic. Just stay where you are, and perhaps we'll both eventually get some rest.'

Sara curled up on the very edge of the mattress, and tensely waited for him to make some other move. He had withdrawn his hand as soon as he had finished speaking, though, and made no other effort to touch her. Very slowly, her tense muscles began to relax and her breathing returned to normal. It looked as if he was going to keep his word, and not try anything.

All the same, she felt very funny, lying there beside him in the darkness. There wasn't any physical contact between them, and yet she was alarmingly aware that he was there. She could hear his quiet, regular breathing; she even thought she could feel the warmth of his body drifting over to her.

Sara swallowed hard, and realised that her throat was uncomfortably dry. She was beginning to wish she had stayed in the chair, but it was too late to move back to it now. Lucas would only laugh at her for being so strait-laced—and for some reason she didn't want him to do that.

Tiredness finally swept over her, and her heavy eyes drooped shut. A couple of minutes later, she was asleep, and she didn't wake up again until the pale light of dawn was shining through the window.

Sara yawned and stretched. Then the back of her hand rubbed against warm, smooth skin that definitely didn't belong to her, and she jumped in surprise.

An instant later, she snatched her hand away. Just for those few moments, she had forgotten where she was—and who she was sharing the bed with!

Then she realised that it wasn't just her hand that had been touching Lucas. Both of them must have moved during the night. They had ended up in the middle of the bed, and were in close contact from head to toe.

'Sorry,' she muttered, and she tried a little frantically to wriggle away from him.

'There's no need to apologise,' Lucas murmured. 'I'm enjoying this very much.'

At that, Sara turned and glared at him. 'Did you move closer on purpose?' she accused.

'Certainly not,' he replied blandly. Then his eyes gleamed. 'Did you?'

'No, I didn't!' Sara denied hotly. She tried to disentangle her leg, which had somehow wound itself around one of his, and felt the colour rise in her face as her skin slid warmly against his.

'Why don't you just lie still for a while, and relax?' suggested Lucas.

'Because I shouldn't—we shouldn't——' she muttered in a voice that was beginning to sound more and more confused.

'But we're not actually doing anything,' Lucas pointed out. 'And I've already promised that I won't pounce on you.'

'But we're together in this bed. And we shouldn't be,' Sara said a little desperately.

'I don't see why not,' came his unperturbed reply. 'It's just another part of getting to know each other.'

'Oh, we've been through all this before,' she said shakily. 'And I don't believe you when you say you didn't move on purpose. I think you did. And that you're thoroughly enjoying every minute of this!'

'I can't deny that,' he admitted. 'But I don't think you can hold me responsible for what I do in my sleep. And we *were* like this when I woke up, Sara.' His gaze deepened. 'It looks as if we're just instinctively drawn towards each other.'

Sara knew perfectly well that she ought to be ignoring all these silly arguments, and instead concentrating on moving away from him. Her limbs felt unexpectedly heavy, though. With a nervous pang, she realised that she didn't actually *want* to move.

As always, Lucas seemed to be frighteningly in tune with her mood. He raised himself on one elbow and loomed over her, so she couldn't see anything except his face. His dark blond hair was even more tousled than usual, his blue gaze was fixed on her with nerve-prickling intensity, and the familiar smile was missing from the corners of his mouth.

'I said that I wouldn't touch you unless you asked me to,' he reminded her softly. His eyes briefly glittered. 'Why don't you ask me to kiss you, Sara?'

Sara tried to think of all the reasons why she shouldn't do such a thing. She was sure there had to be a *hundred* good reasons—but she couldn't seem to remember even one of them. And his mouth was so close, now. So very tempting...

'Why—why don't you kiss me?' she found herself whispering in a voice that didn't sound in the least like her own. Then she couldn't believe that she had actually said it.

Lucas didn't wait for her to frantically take it back, though. Instead, his lips moved over hers with easy familiarity, warm and firm. Sara's muffled objections were lost in their closeness, and then she started to forget *why* she had wanted to object. She moved restlessly as his kiss intensified and felt a light beading of sweat break out on her skin. His own body was hot, and his tongue flickered softly, teasing her to distraction. Sara closed her eyes and gave a faint groan. How had this happened? And why wasn't she trying to put a stop to it?

Then his tongue withdrew and his lips stopped their tantalising pressure. Lucas raised his head and looked down at her, his face slightly flushed with colour and his eyes now burning bright.

'My promise still holds,' he said thickly. 'If you want more, you'll have to ask.'

But Sara just couldn't do it. She knew she should never have come this far. Every time she let Lucas get this close to her, it made it that much harder to keep him at a safe distance in the future.

Her legs were trembling and every inch of her skin felt over-sensitive. With an enormous effort, she shook herself free of him. Then she stared up at Lucas, her eyes huge and green.

'I'm *asking* you to let go of me,' she said tremulously.

For just an instant, she thought he wasn't going to keep his word. He looked as if he wanted to swoop over her and carry her off to some place from which there could never be any return. Then, very slowly, he unlocked his limbs from hers and pulled back.

Sara dragged in a lungful of fresh air. Then, while her mind and body still belonged to her, she hauled herself off the bed, raced into the bathroom, and locked the door.

CHAPTER SEVEN

AFTER a long, cool shower, Sara finally began to calm down. And, once she felt more in control of herself, all the questions began to rush in on her. How had it happened? What on earth had made her behave like that? *Asking* Lucas to kiss her—just the memory brought the colour rushing into her face.

It was with great reluctance that she at last went back into the bedroom. Lucas was standing by the window, and he turned round to face her as she came in.

'I just want to say that what happened was a big mistake——' she began rather stiffly.

'Never mind that,' he interrupted her. 'Give me a few minutes to shower and get dressed. Then we're going out.'

His unexpected announcement made her briefly forget about everything else.

'Going out?' she repeated blankly. 'Where?'

'Back to the ruins. There should be hardly anyone else around this early in the morning. It'll be the perfect time to see them.'

'But——' Sara had been about to say that the last thing she was interested in right now was a lot of old ruins, even if they *were* romantic and magnificent. Then she rather hurriedly stopped herself. It was a good excuse to get out of this hotel room, and she felt that she very much needed to do that. Spending any more time here with Lucas was definitely *not* a good idea. Anyway, perhaps the fresh air would clear away all the highly unsuitable thoughts that seemed to have gathered inside her head.

Lucas emerged from the bathroom in less than ten minutes, caught hold of her hand, and then swept her out of the room. Outside, it was a gorgeous morning, with the early-morning crispness already tempered by the faint warmth of the rising sun. High clouds laced the mountaintops, while the lower slopes shone a fresh bright green in the clear light.

There was no one else walking along the path that led to the site, and when they reached the ruins they found that they had the site to themselves.

Lucas gave a small sigh of satisfaction. '*This* is the way to see Machu Picchu.'

Sara had to admit that he had a point. Walking through the deserted ruins in the early morning sunshine was quite an experience. There was peace and silence all around them, and the feeling that the past and the present had combined, and were living comfortably with one another.

They had strolled to the very far end of the ruins before it occurred to Sara that Lucas was still holding her hand. Somehow, it didn't worry her. She was beginning to accept physical contact between them as normal. At any other time, she would have been distinctly perturbed by that fact. It was hard to worry about anything this morning, though. She wasn't even disturbed by the memory of that kiss he had given her earlier. A kiss which she had actually asked for.

Broken walls rose up behind them and on both sides, providing a sun-trap. Pale golden light shone all around them, and Sara could feel the warmth of it on her skin.

'The Incas worshipped the sun,' Lucas said, in a quiet voice.

'I know,' said Sara, a little dreamily.

'And I worship you,' he said, even more softly.

Her eyes opened very wide. 'You mustn't say things like that!'

'Why not? Don't you like hearing it? Or are you scared of strong emotions?'

Sara realised, rather too late, that she had paid far too little attention to Lucas since she had fled from the bed where he had kissed her. First of all, she had been too preoccupied with her own reactions to the situation. Then she had fallen under the spell of this lost city, as they had wandered around in the tranquil sunshine.

Now, she could see that Lucas didn't look in the least tranquil. The mood of this place certainly hadn't rubbed off on him. Instead, his eyes were much darker than she remembered them, and there was a faint flush of colour along his cheekbones.

'I think we ought to be getting back,' she muttered edgily.

'Not yet.' His voice was husky, and not altogether steady.

'Other people will be arriving here soon.'

'No, they won't. It'll be hours before the tourist train gets here. And most of the people at the hotel aren't even up yet. We'll have this place to ourselves for a while longer.'

He moved closer as he finished speaking, and Sara felt her nerves curl. She had never seen him look quite like this before. The laziness had disappeared from his voice, and the amusement had vanished from his eyes. Instead, they shone with a light which suddenly struck her as very dangerous.

Dangerous to whom? she wondered. Yet, for some reason, she didn't feel as apprehensive as she should have.

Lucas moved still closer, and Sara couldn't figure out why she wasn't backing away. She knew perfectly well that he intended to kiss her, and yet she wasn't doing a single thing to stop it happening. With a jolt of shock, she realised how much she *liked* his kisses.

And yet the kiss, when it finally came, was very different from all the other kisses he had given her. This one was bruising and demanding, as if his self-control was suddenly at a very low ebb. At any other time it would have made her highly nervous. This morning, though, she just didn't care. She was suddenly tired of always being careful and cautious, of never allowing herself to respond with any kind of naturalness.

Lucas lifted his head briefly. 'I want you, Sara,' he told her bluntly. 'And in every way possible.'

She knew she ought to tell him that he couldn't have her, but the words wouldn't seem to come out. He seemed surprised by her silence, and then pleased. He stared down at her for a long time, and Sara felt mesmerised by that dark blue gaze. She didn't know what he could read in her own eyes, but he finally gave a low, satisfied growl. Then he moved in on her.

For the first time, there was very little gentleness in his touch. Sara found, to her astonishment, that it didn't alarm her. As if she were observing someone else instead of herself, she noted how her skin was responding to his searching fingers with burning eagerness, how easily he could make her pulses leap and flare into life.

He leaned closer and kissed the base of her throat, not just once, but over and over, almost compulsively. She lifted her head with the unexpected pleasure of it, and found that the sun was streaming down straight into her eyes, dazzling her. As this man was beginning to dazzle her.

Under his touch, she was changing into a new Sara, a very different Sara. She didn't recognise herself, didn't even know if she liked this new person. But she couldn't seem to stop her from emerging, like a fragile, beautiful butterfly from a dull chrysalis.

And this new Sara didn't protest as Lucas moved even faster than she had expected. He freed her from her T-shirt and the sensible cotton bra, and then just stood and looked at her for a few moments. The expression in his eyes made her skin tingle. She didn't try to cover herself, though. And, when he lowered his head and let his mouth travel purposefully and deliciously over the swell of her breasts, she just stood there and let him do it.

'Do you understand yet, Sara?' Lucas asked huskily, pausing in his delicate exploration for just a moment.

No, she didn't understand. Not any of it. How could she let this stranger do this to her?

Perhaps because he isn't a stranger at all? whispered a dazed voice inside her head.

Sara slowly shook her head. But if that were true—it would mean her whole life would have to change. Was she ready for that yet? Would she *ever* be ready for it?

She desperately needed time to think about all the enormous implications, but Lucas wasn't prepared to wait. He was already pushing her gently down on to the grass. She felt the cool dew against her bare back, in sharp contrast to the heat that was now pouring off his body. He inflicted small, loving bites on her, and her limbs quivered in response. Then she found her own fingers nipping softly in return, as if they ached to return the pleasure.

Lucas shivered. Then his dark blue gaze bore down into hers. 'I knew from the moment I first saw you that you were mine,' he said throatily. 'You knew it too, Sara. But until now, you've been too stubborn to admit it.' His tongue licked her skin gently, and Sara briefly closed her eyes. She was beginning to feel as if he could force her to admit to absolutely anything. 'There were times when I thought you were going to run away from me,' he went on huskily. 'But it wouldn't have mattered. I'd have come after you, and brought you back again.'

Her own eyes were huge and dark now. 'Even if I didn't want to come?' she somehow got out, in a voice that clearly shook.

His mouth relaxed into a confident smile. 'But you *would* have wanted to come,' he said softly, and Sara found she was quite incapable of contradicting him.

The sun beat down a little more brightly, adding to the warmth that already pulsed from their bodies. More and more, this was seeming like a dream to Sara. And if she didn't wake up soon...

You've got to stop this *now*, she silently told herself, as she tried to find a foothold back to reality. Or he won't stop at all. Things are different this morning.

Lucas is different. *You're* different. A few more minutes, and the old Sara might disappear forever...

But it was so hard, especially since Lucas was touching her breasts again. His fingers were almost reverential, moving over their soft swell with delicate precision. Then he gave a small shudder, and his hands began to move more quickly, more intimately, his touch not always so gentle now. Sara found herself fascinated by the pleasure that lapped in their wake. Her mind recognised that it was a frightening, addictive sort of pleasure, but she couldn't seem to draw back from it. He was spinning her off to a magical place, where everything was miraculously possible, and there weren't any restrictions on anything that she said or did.

His skin became hot and damp against her suddenly restless fingertips. He was making no effort to hide his fierce arousal, and she felt her own movements becoming more abandoned in response. An unfamiliar heat poured into her body, as the life-force pulsed urgently between them. Yet the growing urgency of his lovemaking had a seductiveness all of its own and, with a sense of panic, she felt herself being swept way past the point where she could resist it.

Part of her still couldn't believe that this was happening to her. Yet the last of her clothes were now being shed in silence. She knew she ought to protest, and yet she couldn't. Her tongue stuck drily to the roof of her mouth. Only her body seemed capable of any form of communication—and it was telling her something that she had never expected to hear. Lucas *knew* what it was saying, though. Knew, and gave a growl of satisfaction.

Her last intelligible thought was that this was a pagan act on a pagan site. Then Lucas moved possessively over her, and as his hot, heavy weight crushed her she became quite incapable of thinking anything at all.

Instead, a storm of confused sensations swept over her. Slick skin touching slick skin; hardness and warmth; the sound of someone's breath catching sharply. Then her own name, muttered in a hot, husky voice. And, through it all, a growing ache of pleasure that began to pulse in rhythmic waves of growing intensity. Yet it was so much more than simple pleasure. Sara dimly recognised that she was embarking on a journey into the depths of a man's soul. This was a way of knowing him that was more intimate and deeply personal than all the words in the world could ever be.

And it was a journey that was more mysterious and more incredible than she could ever have imagined it would be. The hard, velvety heat of him merged with her own moistness, as he sent them hurtling headlong along a path that her body seemed to have known about and wanted to take for a very long time, but had never dared until this one man had come along and shown her the way.

Then the path ended in a sudden and blinding explosion of delight that drove the breath from her body and left indelible scars on her heart. Confused and dazed and disorientated, Sara seemed to take forever to float back to some semblance of reality. The same sun still shone down on her, and yet her world had changed beyond all recognition. She seemed capable of recording nothing except purely physical sensations. The dampness of the grass against her back, her limp, languid body—and the warmth of the man whose weight still crushed her.

They lay in silence for a very long while. Any words seemed quite unnecessary. Everything that needed to be said had been communicated in other ways.

At last, Lucas raised himself from her. 'Other people will be arriving soon,' he said in a quiet voice. 'We'd better get dressed.'

She allowed him to slide her clothes back on. Then they walked slowly back through the ruins, their fingers lightly linked together. Sara still felt as if she were stepping through a dream—although it was utterly unlike any dream she had ever had before.

After a while, they headed back to the hotel, and had a late breakfast. Sara hadn't expected to be able to eat anything, but to her surprise found that she was starving. She found it hard to look at Lucas, though. An enormous wave of shyness had swept over her, coupled with a growing sense of confusion. Her body was still relaxed, but her mind was in a mess. How could this have possibly happened—and with this man? Her dazed brain wouldn't produce any answers, and the more she tried to find a reason—an excuse—for her behaviour, the more mixed-up she became.

The train back to Cuzco wouldn't be leaving until the middle of the afternoon, which left them with several hours on their hands. In the end, they spent most of it sitting outside in the sunshine and not saying very much to each other. Lucas seemed to understand that she didn't want to talk, that she couldn't find any words to say. And yet, it wasn't an uncomfortable silence. Sara felt as if they could have said nothing at all, and yet still have understood each other perfectly.

The four-hour train ride back to Cuzco seemed to pass incredibly quickly. Sara was still floating on a cloud of relaxation and confusion. It wasn't an entirely unpleasant sensation, and she knew that she wanted to hold on to it for a little while longer. Once she got completely back to reality, she was going to have to think about a lot of things that she didn't want to face just yet.

They took a taxi from the railway station in Cuzco, back to the house that Clarissa had rented. During the short ride, Sara felt her pulses begin to thump rather hard and fast. What would happen when they finally arrived? There would be just the two of them in the house—and Lucas's eyes were beginning to glitter in a way that she already recognised.

The taxi finally came to a halt, and Lucas paid the driver. Then, as they walked through the archway and into the small courtyard, he let his hand rest against her waist in a gesture that was both casual and yet possessive. Sara's skin immediately pulsed with warmth. A couple of days ago, her reaction would have highly alarmed her. This time, she found herself enjoying the sensation.

Her fingers shook a little as she unlocked the front door. She was quite certain that Lucas had noticed, but it didn't seem to matter. All of a sudden, an incredible amount of things didn't seem to matter. It was distinctly unnerving, but that seemed to be the way things were at the moment.

As the front door swung open, they found the light was on in the hall.

'Teresa must have left it on for us,' remarked Lucas. Then he gave a light grin. 'I hope she's also left us some supper. I'm starving.'

'*I* can cook,' Sara said quickly.

'I'm sure you can, sweetheart. I dare say you've got a lot of talents that I haven't even begun to find out about yet,' he went on a little huskily.

Sara felt herself flushing. It was something that she seemed to be doing all the time lately. Where was the cool, controlled Sara who had set out from London only a few days ago?

She couldn't answer that question. In fact, there seemed to be about a hundred questions that she couldn't find answers for at the moment.

Lucas closed the door behind them, and then gently propelled her towards the kitchen. 'Let's have something to eat and drink. Then we can discuss how we want to spend the rest of the evening,' he said, in a tone of voice that made her nerves prickle pleasantly.

Sara pushed open the kitchen door, and then stopped dead. They weren't alone in the house. A slim, fair-haired woman was bustling around the kitchen, preparing some kind of meal.

As she glanced over and saw Sara standing in the doorway, she smiled in greeting. 'Hello, there! You must be Sara. Teresa told me you'd come all this way to see me.' Her gaze slid over the younger girl. 'You've grown up to be quite a beauty! The last time I saw you, you were only two, but even then you were something rather special.'

Sara swallowed hard. 'You're Clarissa?' she finally managed to get out in a stiff voice.

'Of course I am,' agreed the fair-haired woman. 'Don't you recognise me?' Then she gave a wry shrug. 'No, I don't suppose you do. You were so young when I left.'

Sara swallowed again. This was all happening far too suddenly for her. She wasn't *ready* to see Clarissa yet. She hadn't even adjusted to everything else that had happened to her.

But Clarissa wasn't going to go away. She didn't know that Sara needed more time before she had to face all the other problems in her life. She didn't know that, right now, all Sara could seem to think about was Lucas...

Lucas—Sara realised that he was standing silently behind her. She stood aside, so he could come into the kitchen.

'This is Lucas Farraday. He's a—a friend,' she finished a trifle awkwardly.

'Teresa said that you were travelling with someone,' Clarissa said matter-of-factly. 'Very sensible. Women are meant to be able to travel around in these parts quite safely, but you can never be too careful. Anyway, seeing a strange country is much more fun when you've got someone with you, isn't it?' She went over and gave one of the saucepans a stir. 'Are you hungry?' she asked. 'I've been pottering around in the kitchen all evening, trying out some of the local recipes. I can't guarantee that they're completely edible, but you might find something that you like.'

'I could eat just about anything,' grinned Lucas, seating himself at the table. 'Can I help myself?'

'Go ahead,' nodded Clarissa. 'Those,' she pointed to a plate, 'are peppers stuffed with beef and vegetables. There are some chunks of chicken fried in a rather exotic seasoning, and that dish on the end is a kind of local shish kebab. This is a stew,' she explained, stirring the saucepan again. 'It'll be ready in a few minutes, if you want to wait for it.'

'I'll try the stuffed peppers,' Lucas said comfortably. He glanced over at Sara, who had reluctantly slid into the seat opposite him. 'Want to have a go at the chicken? It looks—and smells—delicious.'

Sara's appetite had suddenly gone, though. She put some of the chicken on to her plate, but only nibbled at it. And her gaze kept flicking back to Clarissa.

She hadn't expected to see her quite so soon. She had thought she and Lucas would have a couple of days together, before Clarissa returned. And she had *needed* those couple of days. They would have given her time to try and adjust to the sudden changes in her life. The sight of Clarissa had been an almost physical shock, though. It had brought her very abruptly back to earth, and reminded her of a lot of things that she had wanted to forget for a while longer. Now, she couldn't do that. She only had to look at Clarissa, and she remembered far too much: her reasons for being here, Edward, her old life back in England. And, perhaps most vividly of all, Clarissa reminded her of the legacy that her father *had* left her—a deep fear of getting too closely involved with anyone. Through her father, she had seen the destructive power of love. Seen it, and decided that she wanted nothing to do with it. Only, now she was beginning to break all her own rules...

Clarissa didn't notice the changes that shadowed Sara's face. She was engrossed in her stew, adding small pinches of herbs and seasonings, tasting it, giving small frowns and then chucking in something else. Sara took another half-hearted nibble at her chicken, but couldn't eat any more. Instead, she found herself watching Clarissa with growing intentness, and wondering what it was about this woman that had obsessed her father for so long.

She found it hard to guess at Clarissa's age—late forties, perhaps, or even early fifties. Sara guessed she hadn't changed much over the years. Clarissa still had a good figure, and her hair was cut in a casual tumble of light blonde curls. Perhaps the colour wasn't completely natural any more, but everything else about her seemed quite genuine.

Perhaps the most remarkable thing about Clarissa was that she was so *un*remarkable. Sara hadn't expected that. She had been prepared for some fading *femme fatale*, not someone cheerful and ordinary.

'Well, that's it,' declared Clarissa, giving the saucepan one last stir. 'This stew is about as good as it's going to get. Shall we try it?'

She ladled it out into three dishes, and Sara rather reluctantly tasted hers. Then her eyebrows lifted slightly in surprise. It was delicious!

'If you cook like this all the time, I think I might marry you,' Lucas murmured to Clarissa appreciatively.

Clarissa laughed. 'Sara might have something to say about that!' She ate a little more of the stew, nodded in satisfaction, and then turned back to Lucas. 'Where have the two of you been today? Sightseeing?'

'We've been to Machu Picchu,' replied Lucas. 'We took the early train yesterday, spent the day there, and then stayed overnight.'

'Then you saw the ruins at sunrise?' asked Clarissa with enthusiasm. 'It's a magical place, isn't it, early in the morning when there's no one else around?'

'I thought it was an exceptional experience,' Lucas replied softly, and this time his gaze was locked on to Sara's face.

She felt the colour surge up under her skin, and lowered her head in the hope that neither of them would see it.

To her relief, Clarissa didn't seem to notice. 'I suppose I should ask the two of you what you're doing here,' she chattered on. 'But on the other hand, it's getting late and you're probably rather tired. Perhaps it would be better if we had a talk in the morning. You are staying here tonight, aren't you?'

'If you don't have any objections,' replied Lucas.

'None at all. Do you usually share a room?' Clarissa asked in a practical tone of voice.

'No!' Sara said at once, furious to find that her face was staining bright red again.

Lucas looked at her and fractionally raised one eyebrow. To her utter relief, though, he didn't say anything.

Sara pushed back her chair. 'It's been a long day,' she muttered. 'I think I'll turn in now. I'll—I'll see you in the morning.'

Rather hurriedly, she escaped from the kitchen. She stopped for a few moments at the end of the hall, to try and steady her suddenly shaky legs. Then she jumped violently as a hand touched her shoulder.

'Sure that you don't want to share a room with me?' enquired Lucas in a throaty undertone.

She felt her will-power beginning to drain away, and fought frantically to hang on to it.

I need to get back to normal, she told herself despairingly. But what was normal now? She didn't know, and that was starting to truly terrify her.

'I can't sh-share a room with you,' she stuttered. 'Not here. Not with Clarissa so close.'

'Clarissa won't mind in the least.' Lucas's gaze swept over her assessingly. 'But I get the feeling that Clarissa doesn't have anything to do with this,' he went on evenly. 'I think you're starting to back away from me, Sara.' His dark blue eyes took on a new brightness. 'But I'm not going to let you do it. You do know that?'

'I just want some time to myself,' she mumbled. 'I just want some *time*,' she repeated, a little desperately.

His gaze softened. 'All right, you can have it. I know that I've pushed things too fast. But that's because of the way you get to me.' He moved closer, and for an instant she thought he was going to kiss her. Instinctively, she drew back. If she ever let him get near to her, the last of her self-control would fly right out of the window!

He noticed her withdrawal, and from the look in his eyes it was very obvious that it didn't please him. With an effort, though, he resisted the urge to touch her. He seemed to realise that this was the wrong time for that sort of persuasion.

'We'll talk in the morning, Sara,' he said steadily. Then he turned and walked away from her, leaving her to totter into her room on legs that were openly trembling now.

She shut the door behind her, and wished that it had a lock on it. Although whether it was to keep Lucas out, or to stop her from going to him, she had no idea.

Very slowly, she peeled off her clothes. She knew she ought to shower, but she was suddenly too tired. Exhaustion was threading its way right through her, and she flopped on to the bed with a sigh of relief. Perhaps in the morning all of this would begin to make sense.

Despite her tiredness, though, she couldn't sleep. And as she lay there in the darkness a delayed sense of shock began to creep over her. As if she were watching it on a screen inside her head, she saw the events of early that morning played over in her mind. She saw her own abandoned responses to Lucas's lovemaking, and gave a low moan of disbelief as she realised exactly what she had done. How *could* she have behaved like that? She wasn't the sort of girl who did that kind of thing!

It went a lot deeper than that, though. Sara was finally beginning to realise that this was what she had been running away from for most of her life. She was scared to death of this kind of emotional turmoil. She had seen how it had wrecked her father's life, and she had always been totally determined that it would never happen to her.

She realised now that it was why she had agreed to marry Edward. She was fond of him, but she would never be swept away by him on a great wave of uncontrollable passion. And she didn't want to be swept away. She couldn't—*wouldn't*—live like her father.

And yet—it would mean giving up Lucas. She closed her eyes and tossed restlessly in the darkness. Even if she somehow managed it, could she go back to her old way of life? She had betrayed Edward in the most hurtful way possible. Would he ever forgive her? Would she even be able to find the courage to tell him about it?

Edward—his face briefly floated in front of her, more indistinct than ever. She felt as if he could walk in the door and she wouldn't even recognise him, which made her panic even further.

'You've got to get things together,' she told herself feverishly. 'Sort out this mess you've got yourself into.'

She closed her aching eyes and, although she hadn't expected it, fell into an exhausted sleep only a few minutes later. For the first couple of hours, she moved restlessly around the bed, mumbling out loud now and again. Then she gradually became more still, and towards dawn slept very quietly, not waking again until the sun was shining directly through the window.

As soon as she opened her eyes, she knew that things were different. At some time during the night, as she had slept, she had subconsciously made a decision. The new Sara—the Sara who had frolicked in the damp grass with Lucas and then walked around hand in hand with him all day, like some lovesick teenager—had disappeared. This morning, the old Sara was back again. The Sara who didn't take risks, and who knew how very dangerous it was to allow a deep passion for another human being to take over your life.

After a quick bath, she opened the wardrobe and discovered, to her relief, that her own clothes had been returned. She took out a pleated skirt and a neat white blouse. Then she tied back her hair, clamping down a couple of unruly black curls quite ruthlessly with clips.

She took one last quick glance at herself, and dragged in a deep breath. Then she left the bedroom and made her way steadily to the kitchen.

Her pulses settled down a little when she found that Lucas wasn't there. Clarissa was setting out some ingredients on the table, though, and she looked up and smiled as Sara came in.

'Did you sleep well?' she asked. Then faint surprise showed on her face. 'Good heavens, you don't look quite like the same girl as yesterday! Wouldn't you be more comfortable in casual clothes? I'll lend you some, if you like.'

'Thank you, but these are fine,' Sara replied, in a not very friendly voice. She seated herself at the table. 'I think this would be a good time for us to have a talk.'

'Fire away,' said Clarissa cheerfully. 'You don't mind if I get on with this while we chat, do you? Next to working out new knitting designs, I love cooking, and I'm itching to try out this particular recipe.'

'Perhaps it could wait until a little later?' Sara said rather pointedly.

Clarissa looked disappointed. Then she gave a small sigh. 'I dare say you're right.' She sat down opposite Sara. 'OK, you'd better tell me why you're here. I suppose it has something to do with the death of your father?'

'You know about that?' said Sara in surprise.

'I heard about it through a mutual friend.' Clarissa sighed again. 'Poor man. He must have had such a wretched life.'

'After you walked out, do you mean?' Sara couldn't stop herself from shooting back immediately.

The shadow of an old pain showed in Clarissa's eyes. 'Of course. But I just couldn't stay. I felt so badly about leaving him—and about walking out on you, too. I was so very fond of you. You were a darling little girl. But you're old enough now to understand about these things. You know *why* I couldn't possibly stay.'

'I understand that my father loved you,' Sara said stiffly. 'Was that really so hard to live with?'

Clarissa's eyes opened much wider. They were a clear, light blue, and really rather beautiful. Sara was slowly beginning to understand that a lot of men would find this woman's quiet charms very appealing.

'Your father didn't just love me,' she said. 'He was totally obsessed with me. And then that obsession turned to jealousy. Perhaps I should have seen the signs before we were married, but he must have had it under some sort of control at that time. It wasn't until after the actual wedding that it began to get so completely out of hand.'

'What exactly do you mean—out of hand?'

Clarissa gave a small shiver as if, even now, she didn't like to remember it.

'To start with, he couldn't stand it if I spoke to another man. Even just a polite smile to a sales assistant or the husband of a friend would send him into a frenzy. Then it got to the point where he didn't want me to speak to anyone at all, not even to other women. And he wanted me with him every second of the day, from the moment I got up until the moment I went to bed again. He even took time off work to be with me—heaven knows how he didn't get the sack. I began to feel as if he was completely suffocating me!'

Sara didn't like to think of her father behaving in that frighteningly irrational way. 'Didn't you tell him how you felt?' she asked rather tightly.

'I tried to. But he just wouldn't listen.' Clarissa shook her head slowly. 'When I married your father,

I loved him so much. But by the end of the first year, there were times when I almost hated him. The situation began to get quite nightmarish. I knew that I couldn't go on living like that for very much longer.'

'Couldn't you have persuaded him to get medical help?'

'I only suggested it once—and he nearly went crazy. He said there was absolutely nothing wrong with him, that it was perfectly normal for him to want me all to himself.' Clarissa sadly sighed. 'I just couldn't make him see that his behaviour wasn't normal at all.'

'He really did love you,' Sara said in a low voice.

'I know. That was what made it so awful. But after a year and a half of putting up with that dreadful possessiveness and jealousy, I could see he wasn't going to change. He *couldn't* change—at least, not without professional help, and he was never going to admit he needed that. That was when I decided I had to get out, to save my own sanity.'

'Even though you knew it was going to ruin his life?' Sara's reply was rather sharper than she had intended.

Clarissa's eyes darkened. 'Do you think it was an easy decision? Or one that I made quickly or lightly? But in the end, I knew it was impossible for me to stay. He was turning my life into an absolute hell.'

'If things were that bad, why didn't you divorce him? You're even still using his name!'

'I know.' Clarissa's mouth set into a strange smile. 'And I suppose that's the tragedy of the whole thing. You see, I never actually stopped loving him. There's never been anyone since your father. It was just that I couldn't go on living with him. The kind of obsessive love he had for me is so destructive. If you don't get out, then it kills something inside you.' Her gaze rested on Sara. 'I always felt guilty about leaving *you*, though. I was so fond of you—I wished I could have taken you with me. That would have left your father with nothing, though, and I couldn't have done that to him.'

'I don't think it would have mattered,' Sara muttered, in a voice that was suddenly rough. 'Any love he had was all tied up with you. There was never any left for me.'

Clarissa's expression changed. 'You had a bad time?'

She shrugged. 'He looked after me. That was all, though. *You* were the only one who ever mattered in his life. That's why I'm here,' she went on, her voice a little steadier again now. 'You see, he kept on loving you right up to his death. I've come here to tell you that you're the sole beneficiary of his will. He's left you the house, his possessions—absolutely everything he owned.'

Clarissa slowly sat down. 'I don't want any of it,' she finally said, in a flat voice. 'You can have it. You *should* have it. Oh, the stupid, *stupid* man,' she said very softly. 'He ruined everything that could have been so good.'

Sara started to say something. Then she rather abruptly shut up again. She had come to South America prepared to do battle with this woman for what she had considered to be rightfully hers. Nothing had turned out the way she had expected it, though. And Clarissa was so very different from the picture she had carried in her mind all these years.

'Perhaps we could split it between us,' Sara found herself saying, to her total astonishment. 'That seems only fair——'

'No!' Clarissa interrupted firmly. 'I don't want a single penny of it. It's all yours, Sara. And now, if you don't mind, I think I'd like to be alone for a while.'

Sara got up and quietly left the kitchen, leaving Clarissa sitting there and staring blankly ahead of her, as if she were seeing right back into the past—a past which was both painful and desperately sad.

Sara walked slowly through the hall, so deeply lost in thought that she didn't notice the tall figure standing in the shadow of a nearby doorway. When Lucas's fingers closed over her arm and pulled her, none too gently, into the room beyond, she gave a startled gasp of protest. Then she found herself looking up into his dark blue gaze, and all her nerves were instantly on edge.

'What are you doing?' she said in a voice that no longer sounded quite like her own.

'I want to talk to you,' he replied evenly. 'And I get the feeling that you might be trying to avoid me.' His gaze slid over her clothes and her hair. 'Going back to your old habits, Sara?' he enquired softly.

As always, the way he said her name sent distinct shivers down her spine. She ignored them, though, and kept her face deliberately expressionless.

'This is the way I always dress. I—I happen to like it.'

'You've learnt to like a lot of other things over the past few days,' Lucas reminded her, his eyes never leaving her face for a single moment.

'That was—a mistake,' she got out in a rigid tone.

'It didn't seem like a mistake at the time.' His mouth hardened a fraction 'Do you know what I think?' he said in a voice that suddenly had a dangerous undertone to it. 'I think you've decided to go back to Edward. You're going to throw everything away, Sara, because you're too damned scared to take a few chances.'

'You don't understand——' she began.

'I understand a lot better than you think,' he interrupted harshly. 'You're afraid to let go, to give in to your feelings, in case you turn out like your father!' She went quite white at that, but he ignored it and went on. 'It's much *safer* to get involved with someone like Edward, isn't it? You can be fond of him, without ever running the risk of really *loving* him. And you know all about the dangers of love, don't you, Sara?' he continued relentlessly. 'You've seen how it can ruin people's lives, and so you've decided that it isn't for you. Love doesn't always turn out right—you learnt that from your father. And now Clarissa's confirmed it for you, so you feel justified in taking the coward's way out!'

'You were eavesdropping!' Sara accused in a shaking voice. 'You listened to the conversation I had with Clarissa just now.'

'I listened,' Lucas agreed grimly, and without compunction. 'Sometimes it's the only way to find out things about you, Sara. And at least I'm beginning to understand what makes you tick.'

'You might understand, but it won't do you any good!' she flared back at him. 'You're right, I *am* going back to Edward. He's a kind, decent man. He's my fiancé. He's what I want,' she finished a little wildly.

Ignoring the black, furious expression on Lucas's face, she wrenched herself free of him. Then she rushed back to her bedroom, and frantically began to throw her clothes into her suitcase. She was going home to England, home to Edward. She had to get back to some kind of sanity!

CHAPTER EIGHT

THERE was a small part of Sara—a faint echo of the new Sara—that couldn't quite believe it when Lucas didn't try to stop her from leaving. She had never thought he would let her go so easily.

The old Sara dully accepted it, though. After all, this was what she had wanted, wasn't it? Why should she feel desperately disappointed about it?

It was Clarissa who actually tried to talk her out of going.

'Lucas is such a lovely man,' she said, a little wistfully. 'It'll be a very long time before you find another one like him, Sara.'

'I've got a fiancé back in England,' Sara said stiffly. 'He's also a very nice man.'

'I'm sure he is,' agreed Clarissa. 'But is he like Lucas?'

Sara had to fight hard to stop herself from comparing the two men in her mind.

'No, he isn't,' she said at last. 'And that's why I'm going back.'

Clarissa gave a small sigh. 'I think you're making a very big mistake. But I suppose it's got to be your decision.' Then she gave Sara a rather uncertain smile. 'Would you mind very much if I got in touch with you, when I return to England?' she said a little shyly.

Sara hadn't been expecting that. For a few moments, she didn't know what to say. Then, on impulse, she suddenly nodded. 'Yes, of course you can. I'd—I'd like that,' she finished in a quiet voice.

It didn't take her long to finish packing. The taxi that was going to take her to the airport drew up outside the door, and *still* there wasn't any sign of Lucas. Part of Sara was incredibly hurt, but the other half was deeply relieved. She really didn't think she could cope with a big emotional scene right now.

A sense of numbness began to creep over her during the ride to the airport. Sara welcomed it, and hoped it wouldn't go away too soon. It was such a relief after the highs and lows of the past few days.

She got on to the plane without any trouble, then she held her breath when she found there was an empty seat next to her. This was one of Lucas's favourite tricks, wasn't it? Turning up at the last moment, just when she thought she had finally got rid of him? But a couple of minutes later, a plump, middle-aged lady eased herself into it, and Sara was shocked by the wave of acute disappointment that swept through her. She didn't *want* Lucas to turn up. Of *course* she didn't. That was why she was going back to England, wasn't it—to get away from him? So why was she reacting like this?

The plane finally touched down at Lima, and she went straight to the ticket desk, to try and book a flight back to England. She managed to get a last-minute cancellation and a couple of hours later she was back in the air again. Sara closed her eyes tiredly. At last, she was going home. She had phoned Edward from Lima, while she was waiting to board the plane, and he had promised to meet her at the airport. In just a few hours, everything would be back to normal again.

She slept for a while during the long flight. When she woke up, she turned her head, expecting to find Lucas sitting beside her. For a few moments, she blinked her eyes dozily, and wondered where he was. Then she remembered. He was still in Peru, while she was on her way back to England.

Sara actually groaned out loud. Immediately, the woman sitting next to her turned and looked at her with some concern.

'Are you all right, dear?'

'I'm—I'm fine,' Sara somehow managed to get out. 'Just—just a bit of a headache, that's all.'

The woman signalled to the stewardess. 'This young lady isn't feeling very well,' she said briskly. 'Perhaps some aspirins would help?'

'Of course.' The stewardess gave Sara a friendly smile. 'Anything else I can get you?'

'No, thanks,' muttered Sara, who wished they would just all go away.

When the stewardess came back with the aspirins, Sara quickly gulped them down rather than make a fuss, or draw more attention to herself. Then she sat back and closed her eyes, hoping that they would just leave her in peace.

'I think she needs to rest,' she heard the woman say to the stewardess, in a low voice. 'She looks very pale and tired. Too much travelling, I expect.'

Too much Lucas Farraday, Sara silently corrected her. She had broken all her own rules, and now she was paying the price.

The flight seemed to go on forever, and yet she didn't mind. When it finally came to an end, she would have to return to her old life again, and just the thought of it utterly depressed her.

You'll be fine once you see Edward again, she told herself doggedly. You'll forget all about the last few days—about South America—and about Lucas.

By the time the plane at last landed, she was genuinely exhausted. She collected her luggage and went through Customs in a daze. Then she stared at the small group of people who were waiting for the passengers off the plane. Where was Edward?

A pleasant-looking man took a couple of steps towards her.

'Sara?' he said.

Sara blinked at him. Then his features slowly slid into focus, and she realised that she recognised them.

'Edward,' she said in a shaky voice. He was familiar, and yet somehow looked like a stranger. Anyone could have had those rather pale eyes, that thin mouth, the well-brushed brown hair.

She stood there, staring at him, for what seemed like ages. He smiled back at her, and didn't seem to notice that anything was wrong.

'Let me take your case,' he offered. 'The car's waiting outside.'

Sara released her case to him, but her legs wouldn't seem to move. She was suddenly so tired that she couldn't seem to take a single step. And there was an awful prickling behind her eyes——

Before she could stop them, the tears began to flow. Oh, why did this keep happening to her? she wondered a little despairingly. Before she had met Lucas, she had hardly *ever* cried. Now, she seemed to keep doing it all the time—and in public, which was even worse.

The tears streamed down her face, and she fumbled around awkwardly for a handkerchief. Edward's hand moved uncertainly towards her, as if he wanted to pat her arm. Then he pulled back again and shuffled his feet uneasily, obviously highly embarrassed by this unexpected scene.

'I'm sorry——' she sniffled.

'That's all right,' he said uncomfortably. 'Jet-lag, I expect. It affects different people in different ways.' He glanced round. 'Look, we'd better get out of here,' he muttered. 'Everyone's watching——'

Lucas wouldn't have cared if the whole world had been watching, Sara found herself thinking. He'd have simply taken me in his arms and given me a huge hug until I felt better——

Then she very hurriedly put a brake on her thoughts. Lucas wasn't here. He was *never* going to be here. Edward was, though, and she had better stop embarrassing him. Anyway, she expected Edward was right, and it *was* only jet-lag that was making her feel so awful.

Edward whisked her back to her house—which would now be hers forever, since Clarissa had waived all claim to it. He carried her suitcase into the hall. Then he stood there, looking a little indecisive.

'I'd better go,' he said at last. 'I expect you want a good sleep after that long journey. I'll ring you tomorrow and see if you're feeling better. If you are, you can tell me what happened in South America.'

For just a moment, Sara jumped guiltily. Then she realised that he was only referring to her meeting with Clarissa.

'That sounds fine,' she said in a low voice. 'Good night, Edward.'

She had tried to inject some warmth into her tone, but only managed to sound very tired and somehow extremely indifferent. Fortunately, Edward was already turning away and walking off down the path.

Sara didn't bother to unpack, or even undress. Instead, she went up to her room, flopped down on to the bed, closed her eyes and was asleep within seconds.

When she woke up again, the sun was shining through the window and the birds were singing. She took a quick glance at her watch, and then groaned. She had been asleep for hours!

She went over to the window and took several deep breaths of sweet, fresh air, which gradually cleared her fuzzy head. Then she gazed down at the garden, which was rather overgrown, but looked comfortingly familiar. And now it was all hers, along with the house. The thought should have cheered her up, but it didn't. She almost wished she had let Clarissa have the house. That way, she wouldn't have gone to South America—wouldn't have met Lucas Farraday.

A little angrily, Sara shook her head. She had to stop thinking about him! He was out of her life now. It was *Edward* who had to occupy her thoughts from now on.

Over the next few days, she made a determined effort to get back to her old way of life. She returned to her job at the bank; but, where she had always enjoyed it before, it now struck her as rather dull. Her friends—most of them older than herself—suddenly seemed middle-aged and distinctly staid. Even Edward——

Edward was *not* middle-aged. And he was *not* dull, she told herself staunchly. She would soon adjust and be happy again. She was bound to be unsettled by that disturbing trip half-way round the world.

But by the end of the second week she had to admit that things hadn't improved. In fact, they were getting worse. Sara was getting slightly panic-stricken by this time. She hadn't known it would be this awful.

For perhaps the hundredth time, she glanced down at Edward's ring, now safely back on her finger again. Part of the problem, of course, was her over-whelming sense of guilt. She had betrayed Edward in the worst way possible, and so far she had been too much of a coward to tell him about it. Yet, if she told him, she was sure she would lose him—and then she would have nothing and no one. She was perhaps scared of that most of all, and so she hung on, and suffered, and tried to pretend that everything would turn out all right in the end.

At the end of the third week, Edward rang her at the bank. It was unusual for him to do that—he strongly disapproved of personal contact during working hours. Just for once, though, he had relaxed his own rules since he wanted to give her some good news. He had been invited to a weekend in the country, and the invitation included a friend.

'I know you've been a bit off colour since you went to South America to see your stepmother,' he went on. 'Probably some bug you picked up there,' he added sympathetically. 'I know what the hygiene's like in these places. This is exactly what you need, darling. A couple of days in the country, where you can get some rest and fresh air.'

'Who's invited you?' she asked, without too much enthusiasm.

'A man called Barrington—he's very influential in certain financial circles. Apparently, he's putting together some sort of consortium, and he's invited down several people he thinks might be interested.' Edward's voice was deliberately low-key, but she could tell that he was highly pleased at having been included.

'If everyone's going to talk business, I'll feel rather out of it,' said Sara.

'Of course you won't,' Edward replied firmly. 'Everyone will be bringing along their wives. Weekends like these are social occasions, as much as anything else.'

'I'm not a wife,' Sara pointed out.

Edward gave a rather exaggerated sigh. 'Sara, are you deliberately being difficult? I want to take you with me because I think it'll be good for you. And please remember that this weekend could be *very* important for me. I'll be meeting some very well-connected people, and that could open some important doors.'

Sara knew that he was reminding her that, as his fiancée, she had certain obligations. She somehow stifled a faint sigh; then she tried to sound enthusiastic. 'Of course I'll come, Edward. What time do you want to leave?'

'Can you get away early on Friday?'

'I'll try.'

'Then I'll pick you up around four. Bye for now, darling.'

Sara put down the receiver. About the last thing she felt like right now was a weekend in the country with a lot of city whiz-kids, who would talk business all day and half the night. She supposed she owed it to Edward to go with him, though.

On Friday, Edward arrived at four o'clock precisely. Sara was waiting for him, her bag packed with a selection of clothes that she hoped would be suitable for this type of weekend.

The traffic out of London was heavy, but moving steadily. She already had a faint headache, and had the feeling it was going to get a lot worse. She glanced at Edward sitting beside her in his well-cut conservative suit, and for just a moment wondered what she was doing here with him. Then she looked at the ring on her finger, and suddenly knew that she couldn't go on like this. Somehow, she was going to find time this weekend to tell Edward what had happened in South America. She couldn't keep all these secrets from him any longer. If he broke off their engagement, she would just have to find some way of coping with it. However it turned out, she couldn't end up feeling any worse than she did right now.

She felt slightly better once she had made that decision. They were about an hour out of London now, and driving through gently rolling countryside. The sun glinted through the trees, the sky overhead was a clear pale blue, and it seemed very peaceful in contrast to the city they had so recently left behind.

About a quarter of an hour later, Edward turned the car through a wide gateway. A short drive curved its way past a wide area of grass studded with majestic copper beeches, stately oaks and elegant birches. Then Edward's dark BMW drew smoothly to a halt alongside a line of equally expensive cars, parked outside a staggeringly beautiful house.

It was long and low, and perfectly proportioned. Gold brickwork glowed in the late sunshine, and more light was reflected from the long lines of windows. Ornamentation had been kept to a minimum—the lines of the house itself were so clean and flowing that any decoration would have been superfluous.

Edward was looking at it without enthusiasm, though. 'It's very plain,' he remarked.

'Oh, no, it's perfect,' breathed Sara. 'Does it belong to this man, Barrington, who's invited us for the weekend?'

'I suppose so.' Edward got out of the car. Then he came round and opened the door for her. 'I prefer something Georgian,' he went on, still looking at the modern lines of the house with some disapproval. 'Traditional styles are a much better form of investment.'

Sara gave a resigned shrug. Edward liked nice things, but he always had to put a value on them.

'Let's go in,' she said. 'I want to see what the interior's like.'

As they approached the front entrance, the door opened and a tall, lean man came out to meet them.

'You must be Edward and Sara,' he said, in a distinct American accent. Then, seeing the surprise on Sara's face, he grinned. 'I'm not a mind-reader,' he added. 'It's just that everyone else is already here, so I guessed who you were by the process of elimination!' He turned to Edward, and shook his hand. 'I hope you have a great weekend. I'm Mike Barrington. Can I call you Ed?'

Sara very nearly giggled out loud at the pained look that crossed Edward's face.

'I'd prefer it if you called me Edward,' he said stiffly.

'That's fine by me, Edward,' said Mike, with another cheery grin. 'Bring your bags in, and I'll show you to your rooms.'

Inside, the hall was large and spacious. Arched doorways led off it to the other rooms on the ground floor, while a wide staircase wound itself elegantly up to the first floor.

Sara and Edward followed Mike Barrington up the stairs. He bounded on ahead, which gave Edward the chance to speak to Sara in a low voice.

'I didn't know he was going to be an American.'

'They can be very nice, you know,' she whispered back, trying very hard to keep a straight face. 'Almost civilised—or so I've heard.'

'Don't be flippant,' Edward said shortly. 'You know very well what I mean.'

Sara stopped looking amused and instead gave a faint sigh. Yes, she knew what he meant. Edward didn't really approve of anyone unless they looked, sounded and dressed like him, and came from the same sort of background.

Mike showed Edward into one of the rooms on the first floor. 'This is yours,' he said. 'I hope you find it OK. If not, just give me a shout.'

'I'm sure it will be fine,' Edward said politely.

Mike turned to Sara. 'You're in the east wing, I'm afraid.' His eyes twinkled. 'I hope that won't be inconvenient? If it is, I could try and move you nearer to Edward.'

'That won't be necessary,' Edward cut in, in a cold tone. 'Sara and I are only engaged, not married.'

Mike shrugged. 'It's the same thing, as far as a lot of people are concerned.'

'Not for us,' Edward replied icily. Then he turned to Sara. 'I'm going to unpack and change. I'll see you at dinner.' He turned back to Mike. 'What time is the evening meal?'

'Around eight o'clock, probably. Don't bother to dress up, though. It's going to be a very casual affair.'

Sara could see that this weekend wasn't going to turn out at all the way Edward had expected. In fact, he looked as if he was wishing that he could go back home right now. That wouldn't have been polite, though, and Edward was always very courteous.

Mike picked up Sara's bag. 'Come on, then,' he said. 'Let's go and find your room.'

She followed him along a corridor that had long windows all down one side, which gave them stunning views of the grounds.

'This is a fantastic house,' she said admiringly. 'Is it yours?'

'No, it's mine,' said a very familiar voice from just behind her.

Sara felt as if she was hallucinating. It had sounded like—— It couldn't be, though. It couldn't! All the same, she stood very still. And she didn't dare turn round.

'I think that this is where I leave you,' said Mike, with a grin. 'See you later, Sara. And have a great weekend.'

He put down her bag, and walked off. A moment later, Lucas picked it up. Then he took hold of Sara's arm. 'Your room is this way,' he said, gently nudging her forward.

'I don't believe this,' she croaked.

'Of course you do,' he said in a relaxed voice. 'I think you've spent the last three weeks waiting for me to turn up.'

'I haven't!' she lied furiously.

'Then you should have done. You didn't really think I was going to let you just walk out of my life, did you?' he asked reasonably.

Sara wished her legs would stop shaking so very badly. If they kept it up much longer, he was bound to notice.

'I'm back with Edward,' she said in a tense voice. 'Or has that small fact escaped your attention?'

'Nothing you do escapes my attention,' Lucas said softly. 'And as for being back with Edward—I don't think that'll turn out to be a very permanent arrangement.'

'Yes, it will!' yelled Sara. Then she somehow got hold of herself again. 'I'm going to marry him,' she said stubbornly. 'I *am*.'

'Of course you're not,' Lucas replied, quite unperturbed by her outburst. 'But you needed to go back to him for a while—just to realise how very unsuited the two of you are. I hated letting you go, of course,' he went on, 'but I knew I could trust Edward not to touch you. You'd already told me that he's a gentleman.'

'And you're certainly not!'

'No, I'm not,' he agreed cheerfully. 'I go all out for what I want—and I want you,' he finished in a very different tone of voice, his dark blue eyes glittering now in a way that she remembered only too well.

He put down her small case, and opened the door in front of them. 'This is your room,' he went on. 'It's one of the best in the house. It's also a very long way from Edward's—but quite close to mine,' he added with a wicked grin.

'I'm not staying here,' she declared immediately. 'I'm going back to London right now.'

Lucas shook his head regretfully. 'I don't think you should do that. You don't want to ruin Edward's business prospects, do you?'

She stared at him in disbelief. 'Are you blackmailing me?' she got out at last. 'Are you saying that, if I leave, you'll cut Edward out of any deals that are made this weekend?'

'That's exactly it,' Lucas agreed without compunction. 'And you wouldn't want to be responsible for Edward losing out on some very profitable business opportunities, would you?'

'That is totally despicable,' she said icily.

'I know,' he sighed, but without any genuine trace of regret. 'But how else am I going to keep you here for the weekend, Sara?'

Sara was torn between her compulsive need to get away, and the knowledge that, if she grabbed her bag and ran, she would be harming Edward.

'All right, I'll stay,' she said at last, in a strained voice. 'But only for Edward's sake!'

'I'll leave you to unpack and freshen up, then,' Lucas replied in a satisfied voice. 'See you later, Sara.'

As always, he said her name in a way that made her nerves curl. Very hurriedly, she closed the door before he could see the colour rise in her face. Then she slumped against it and took a couple of deep breaths, trying to steady the erratic thumping of her heart.

She still couldn't quite believe it. She was in *Lucas's house*. He had deliberately lured her here, and then made sure that she couldn't get away for the next couple of days. At least, not without harming Edward, and she was determined not to do that. She already felt guilty enough about the way she had betrayed him.

Her headache was much worse now, the pain thudding dully against her temples. For a few moments, she wondered if she could use it as an excuse for getting out of dinner. Then she gave a despairing sigh. She could hardly use a headache as an excuse for staying out of sight for the next couple of days! She had better just march down there and get it over with.

She spent much longer than usual getting ready. She slapped on a lot of make-up to disguise the fact that she looked horribly pale. Then there was the question of what to wear. Mike had said to dress casually, but she knew Edward would disapprove of that. In the end, she compromised, and wriggled into a dress that was the same green as her eyes, but plain enough to be suitable for just about any occasion. Then, on legs that still weren't entirely steady, she made her way downstairs.

There were about a dozen people in the dining-room. As soon as she came in, Mike came over and caught hold of her arm. 'The most gorgeous girl in the room,' he said appreciatively. 'No wonder Lucas is pining for you.'

Sara swallowed hard. 'You—you know about—about me and Lucas?' she stuttered.

'Of course. Lucas and I go way back. I know him as well as I know anyone. As soon as he got back from South America, I knew something was wrong. Off his food, pacing around all hours of the day and night, growling at everyone—he had all the symptoms of someone who's been hit by love. What I *can't* understand,' went on Mike thoughtfully, 'is how you can possibly prefer that guy, Edward. He's got nice manners and he dresses well, but he doesn't seem to have a lot else going for him. Lucas might be a bit unconventional at times, but you'd have a lot more fun with him.'

'I really don't think it's any of your business,' Sara snapped tensely.

'You're right,' agreed Mike cheerfully. 'I won't mention it again. Come and meet everyone.'

Names and faces floated through Sara's head as Mike paraded her around the room, introducing her to the rest of his guests. Then they floated straight out again. She couldn't think clearly this evening; her aching head seemed full of cotton wool. She wasn't even sure she was making any sense as she mumbled replies to people's questions. And all the time her gaze was darting around a little frantically, looking for Lucas. She only relaxed a fraction when she realised that he wasn't in the room.

He came in just after the first course of the evening meal had been served. Sara nearly choked on her soup, which she had already been having problems in getting down.

'Sorry I'm late,' Lucas apologised to everyone in general, as he seated himself directly opposite Sara. 'I was waiting for a phone call.'

'Business or pleasure?' enquired the rather elegant woman sitting next to him, with an amused smile.

'Business, of course,' replied Lucas. His gaze shifted lazily over to Sara. 'I'm not interested in pleasure right now—unless it's with the right person.'

Sara's gaze flew down to her soup and then fixed there. Perhaps if she didn't look at him, she could pretend he wasn't even there!

That didn't turn out to be a very practical solution to her problems. She could still *hear* him, and just the sound of his voice brought back so many memories that her throat closed up completely and she couldn't eat a single thing.

'No appetite this evening?' enquired Lucas, after a while.

Sara raised her head and found that everyone else at the table was engaged in conversation. For these few moments, they could talk freely.

'Why have you put Edward right at the far end of the table?' she hissed at him. 'Why isn't he sitting next to me?'

'Because I intend to keep the two of you as far apart as possible during this weekend,' Lucas replied calmly.

'It won't do you any good!'

He shrugged. 'Maybe. Maybe not. But at least it'll make me feel better, not having to see the two of you together.' He pushed her glass towards her. 'If you won't eat, why don't you try some wine?' he suggested. 'You're very uptight this evening. Edward seems to do that to you.' His gaze darkened. 'You were a lot more relaxed when you were with me,' he murmured.

'I don't remember that,' she said instantly.

'You remember every single second of it,' came his slightly husky response. 'Do you know what your problem is, Sara?' His gaze locked on to hers and relentlessly held it. 'You're afraid of falling in love. You're fighting it tooth and nail, but it's a fight that you just can't win. That's why I invited you here this weekend—to prove it to you.'

'No!' she said, so sharply that a couple of people turned their heads and looked at her. She coloured slightly. 'No,' she repeated, in a much quieter voice, but sounding no less determined.

'You might not have a choice, Sara,' Lucas pointed out softly. 'It might have already happened.'

She didn't even answer him. Instead, she stared fiercely at her plate and deliberately shut his words right out of her head. Just two more days, she told herself. Two more days—that was only forty-eight hours. Then she could get away from here—and from Lucas. Only, right now, those forty-eight hours stretched ahead of her like forty-eight weeks.

When the meal was over, she escaped as soon as she could, pleading a quite genuine headache. Edward didn't seem to mind that she was leaving him on his own. He was deep in conversation with two other men, discussing the financial details of some deal that was being planned. He hardly seemed to hear her when she came over to say good night.

She went up the stairs, lightly rubbing her aching temples. It was such a relief to get away from that brightly lit room and all those cheerful, talkative people. When she reached the door of her room, she finally began to relax a fraction. This was what she badly needed—some peace and quiet. She might even eventually be able to get some sleep.

Sara opened the door and switched on the light. Then her breath caught in her throat, because Lucas was sitting on the edge of the bed, waiting for her.

CHAPTER NINE

'GET out!' Sara said in a choked voice.

'In just a few minutes,' Lucas replied evenly. 'First of all, we have to talk.'

'About what?' she flung at him a little wildly. 'The way you tricked me into coming here?'

He shrugged. 'It wasn't exactly a trick. Mike's put together a very good deal, and he's looking for financing. He asked if he could use my house for the weekend, to entertain prospective backers, and I agreed, but only on the condition that I could invite you and Edward. Mike's an excellent businessman,' he went on. 'And he's got some very influential contacts in the States. Edward could come out of this very well. It certainly won't be a wasted weekend, as far as he's concerned.'

'You're trying to buy him off?' said Sara in a horrified tone.

'Not exactly.' Lucas suddenly grinned. 'Just offering him some compensation. It's the least I can do, after taking you away from him.'

'You haven't taken me away from anyone!' Sara yelled at him.

'Not yet,' agreed Lucas. 'But I intend to keep working at it.' Then a faint scowl crossed his face. 'We wouldn't be having all these problems if it weren't for your father. This entire situation is his fault. He should have put his own problems behind him, and taken time to teach you that there's a huge difference between obsession and genuine love.'

'I know everything that I need to know,' Sara insisted stubbornly. '*You're* the one who's causing all the problems in my life.'

'And I intend to cause a few more before this weekend is over,' promised Lucas, making Sara's skin prickle with pure apprehension. 'But I feel much better about the situation now that I've actually met Edward.'

'What on earth do you mean?' she demanded.

'Believe it or not, I felt rather guilty about Edward. For all I knew, he might have been madly in love with you. He might even have been completely broken up when you left him.'

'I'm not going to leave him,' Sara said heatedly. 'And he *is* in love with me.'

'No, he isn't,' Lucas replied calmly. 'He's certainly fond of you, but he doesn't love you. As far as he's concerned, you'll be the sort of wife he wants, and so he's satisfied. At least, he *thinks* you'll be the sort of wife he wants, but that's because he doesn't know you very well. If you'd gone ahead and married him, the poor man would probably have been in for quite a few shocks. On the other hand,' he went on reflectively, 'I'm completely shockproof. And you're *exactly* the sort of wife that I want.'

Sara clapped her hands over her ears. 'Stop this,' she got out through gritted teeth. 'Just stop it!'

Lucas got up and walked over to her.

'I've no intention of stopping,' he told her, and this time there was a distinct edge to his voice. 'Your father ruined his own life—but I'm damned if he's going to ruin yours, or mine. You're going to get over this fear of falling in love, Sara, even if I have to spend the rest of my life teaching you how to do it.'

'I'm already in love,' she insisted a little frantically. 'With Edward!'

'No, you're not,' Lucas said with complete assurance. 'You're fond of Edward. You feel comfortable with him. But you're in love with me.'

'You're so arrogant! I suppose you think you're irresistible.'

'No. But I understand you, Sara. And I know what you want——' His lips closed over hers before she had time to protest. The familiar touch of his mouth seemed to open up a floodgate of memories, and almost immediately she began to drown in them.

'Let go of me,' she muttered in a ragged voice, while she was still capable of getting the words out.

'Not just yet.' There was no amusement in his voice now. 'This is too important. I want you to understand what you're trying to throw away.'

He bent his head. As his kisses fringed the nape of her neck, she shivered. Then she shivered all over again as his fingers slid over the curve of her breast.

'This isn't everything,' she somehow managed to whisper. 'There are more important things than m-making love.'

'Of course there are,' he agreed throatily, to her astonishment. 'But it's one way of communicating. And you're saying a great deal to me right now, Sara.'

'What—what sort of things?' She knew she shouldn't have asked, but somehow she couldn't help it.

His hands moved over her with complete assurance. 'That you're not afraid of me. That this feels right to you.' His thumb caressed one hardened nipple.

'And that you do want me,' he finished much more huskily.

An enormous shudder ran through her. Quite suddenly, all the things she had been trying to run away from for so long seemed to catch up with her, and she felt herself beginning to crumple. Her eyes grew wide and feverish, and she shook her head a little despairingly.

'But what if I *am* like my father?' she muttered. 'I think I might be. Do you know what happened to me in South America?' she went on, in a voice that openly trembled. 'I started to realise that you were the first thing I looked for when I got up in the morning. I knew that if I stayed near you much longer, I wouldn't ever want to let you out of my sight.' The confession just kept tumbling out of her, and she couldn't stop it. 'You might not mind that at first, but eventually you'd get to hate it—as Clarissa did. And anyway, I don't want to be that way. It's too frightening—I can't live like that!'

Abruptly, she stopped, knowing that she had said far too much. Lucas didn't look concerned at her outburst, though. Instead, he simply wrapped his arms around her shivering body and held her very tightly until the trembling eased a little.

'I don't give a damn *how* much you love me,' he said softly. 'And you're only scared of the way you feel because it's all new to you.'

Almost violently, Sara shook herself free of him. 'But I don't want to feel this way,' she insisted. 'And you've no right to make me!'

He gave an odd little shrug. 'What else can I do? I've got to find some way of getting through to you.'

'You could just leave me alone and let me get on with my life!'

'I can't do that. But I'll tell you what I *will* do.' Sara waited tensely. 'I'll give you the rest of tonight to think things over. Heaven knows, I didn't intend to, but I don't think you can cope with any more pressure right now. And in the morning, I want you to make some sort of decision. But make sure that it's the right decision, Sara,' he warned a little grimly. 'Or you'll end up driving both of us completely crazy.'

With that, he rather abruptly left her. Sara sank weakly down into the nearest chair, and didn't move for ages. This was all getting too much for her. Lucas turning up like this, and making these demands on her. And what if she didn't give in to them? Was he going to haunt her for the rest of her life?

Somehow, she managed to get from the chair to the bed. She curled up in a small ball, and then closed her eyes. He had told her to think things over, but she couldn't. Her mind seemed to be a total blank. Too much had happened in too short a space of time. Her father's death; the trip to South America; meeting Lucas; trying so hard to love Edward . . .

At that, her eyes suddenly shot open again. *Trying* to love Edward? Had it really been that difficult? And had she really ever succeeded?

Her tired brain wouldn't supply any answers. Instead, it seemed to switch itself off completely. A few seconds later, her eyes drooped shut again and she drifted into a restless sleep.

Sara woke up in the morning with a deep sense of foreboding. Then she remembered everything that had happened last night and, with a small groan, she buried her face in the pillow. Lucas was waiting for her decision. Edward was waiting for her to join him for breakfast. And right now she didn't want to see anyone at all.

She glanced at her watch. It was still early. Probably no one else would be up yet. She got out of bed and took a quick shower. Then, when she was dried and dressed, she let herself out of the bedroom and went downstairs. The house still seemed very silent. The rest of the houseguests must have stayed up fairly late last night, and be sleeping it off this morning.

She decided that she needed some coffee—*strong* coffee. She definitely needed to be wide awake. Who knew what she was going to have to cope with today?

It took her quite some time to find the kitchen. While looking for it, though, she saw much of the ground floor of the house, and was impressed all over again by the design. This was the kind of house that would be very easy to live in. She found herself wondering how long Lucas had owned it; then she rather rapidly clamped down on her thoughts. She didn't want to think about Lucas at all until it was absolutely necessary.

She finally found the kitchen quite by chance. She pushed open a door on her left, and there it was. It wasn't empty, though. A tall woman, maybe in her late fifties, was bustling around in a very purposeful way.

'Oh—sorry—I didn't mean to disturb anyone,' apologised Sara. Then her gaze fixed curiously on the woman. There was something very familiar about her dark blonde hair, and the deep blue of her eyes.

The woman was looking back at her with equal curiosity. 'I think I know who you are,' she said at last, her face breaking into a friendly smile. 'You must be Sara.'

Sara blinked. 'How do you know that?' Then she stared at the woman even more closely. 'I feel as if I should know you,' she said slowly.

'I expect you do,' replied the woman cheerfully. 'I'm Lucas's mother.'

'Lucas's——' Sara swallowed very hard. 'What— what are you doing here?' she finally managed to get out. 'Do you live here?'

'Heavens, no,' said his mother briskly. 'But I run a small catering organisation. We provide food for parties, weddings, and all kinds of social occasions. When Mike Barrington set up this weekend, he asked me if I'd take over the catering. I agreed at once— for one thing, I hoped it would give me the chance to meet you. And here you are,' she beamed, obviously very pleased with the way things had turned out.

'Lucas told you about me?' said Sara a little shakily.

'He didn't have to. As soon as he came back from South America, I knew he'd met someone. I finally managed to wheedle a few details out of him, and you sounded so interesting that I decided I wanted to see you for myself.'

'Interesting?' Sara echoed faintly. 'Me?'

'Of course. Lucas would never fall so hard for someone who was boring. And you *look* as gorgeous as he described you. I'm really very pleased with the choice he's made,' said his mother, with some satisfaction. 'And relieved! I was beginning to think he was never going to find someone who suited him.'

'And what if *he* doesn't suit *me*?' Sara asked, rather more sharply than she had meant.

'Oh, I'm sure he does,' replied his mother, giving a dismissive wave of her hand. 'Lucas is really too likeable for his own good. And you'll find him very easy to live with. He's basically a very uncomplicated man. He's got rather a lot of money, of course, but I don't suppose you'll find that too much of a problem. And you look like a sensible girl. You won't spend the whole lot in one go.'

'There is one small problem,' Sara pointed out, in a rather stiff voice. 'I already have a fiancé!'

His mother seemed completely untroubled by that piece of information. 'Yes, Lucas did mention that,' she said airily. 'But I gather that your engagement's all been a bit of a mistake. We all make them. The thing is to recognise our mistakes and put them right before any real harm is done.'

Before Sara could say anything, the kitchen door burst open and two girls about her own age rather breathlessly came in.

'Is she here?' asked one of them rapidly. 'Have you seen her yet?' Then, as Lucas's mother gestured pointedly towards Sara, she pulled a face. 'Whoops,' she said ruefully. 'Put my foot in it again!'

'These are my two daughters,' said Lucas's mother, with a grimace, 'Josie and Ellen. Believe it or not, Josie is married with twin boys, and Ellen's a fully-qualified architect. Unfortunately, they both still behave like sixteen-year-olds at times!'

'Sorry,' said Josie, with a cheerful grin at Sara. 'It's just that we were dying to see you. You're the first female who's ever managed to get her hooks into our brother, and we wanted to know how you managed it!' She studied Sara frankly. 'Thank heavens you haven't turned out to be some blonde bimbo. It's always a worry when you've got an unmarried older brother. I mean, what if he gets hitched to someone totally unsuitable? Ellen and I would have to spend the rest of our lives pretending to like her, and it really would be an awful strain!' She turned to Ellen. 'I think Sara looks completely suitable, don't you?'

'Don't let my sister embarrass you,' said Ellen, with a smile at Sara. 'She's really very nice, when you get to know her.'

Ellen was obviously the quieter of the two. Now that Sara had had a chance to look at her more fully, she could see that she was older than she had thought at first. Then Sara remembered something else that Lucas's mother had said.

'You're an architect?' she recalled. 'I wonder—did you design this house?'

'Yes, I did,' nodded Ellen. 'It was my first big commission. I was terrified in case I loused it up! Luckily, Lucas was very pleased with it.'

'So he should be,' Sara said at once. 'It's an absolutely beautiful house.'

'This girl has got marvellous taste,' declared Josie. 'She's going to make a perfect sister-in-law!'

'I haven't—I mean, we haven't——' began Sara a trifle awkwardly.

'What Sara's trying to say is that there are still a few things that have to be settled,' said Lucas's mother firmly. 'So why don't we leave her alone for a while, so she can get them sorted out?' She turned to Sara. 'You'd better make a run for it, before they start on you again,' she said good-humouredly. 'I expect we'll see you again later.'

Sara escaped from the kitchen while she had the chance. She certainly hadn't expected to be confronted with the Farraday family *en masse* this morning! Really, there seemed no escape from the wretched man. If he wasn't pursuing her in person, then he was sending his relatives after her!

On the other hand, was she still totally determined to get away from him? She gave a small groan. Oh, she was getting so confused! She had thought her future was all planned. Now, she was being offered an alternative—and what a beguiling alternative it was!

She decided she needed some fresh air—and some solitude. It was so hard to think straight with all these Farradays around.

She let herself out through the back entrance, and walked slowly through the garden. The grounds of the house stretched enticingly out in front of her, and she was just about to set off on a long stroll when she saw a familiar figure sitting on the wooden bench at the end of the path.

It was Edward. A huge pang of guilt shot through Sara as she saw him. He might not be a very sensitive man, but he certainly didn't deserve to be treated the way that she had treated him.

Her feet dragging slightly, she made her way towards him. As she drew nearer, he lifted his head. Then, when he saw who it was, he got to his feet.

Sara looked at him and saw a pleasant-looking man who really didn't seem to have anything at all to do with her. For a moment, she was completely confused; then there suddenly seemed to be a great flash of revelation inside her head. Everything clicked magically into place, and the whole crazy mess made perfect sense. She didn't love Edward. She had *never* loved Edward. And, now that she was seeing clearly for perhaps the first time in her adult life, she marvelled that she had ever thought of marrying him. They didn't belong together. The extraordinary thing was that she hadn't been able to see it before.

She walked over to him. Then, when she was standing just a couple of feet in front of him, she slid the ring off her finger and held it out to him.

'I'm sorry, Edward,' she said, her voice apologetic but quite calm and sure. 'I can't marry you. I have to give you back your ring.'

For just a moment, he hesitated. Then he took it from her.

Sara looked at his face. 'You don't seem very surprised.'

'I don't think I am.' Almost absently, he slid the ring into his pocket. Then he gave a small frown. 'To be honest, Sara, it's almost a relief. These last few days, it's occurred to me that we're not entirely suited. Perhaps I should have spoken to you about this before, but I didn't want to hurt your feelings. The truth is, though, that I feel you're a little too young for me. And perhaps a little too irresponsible.'

Sara gave him a faint smile. 'Young?' she echoed. 'Irresponsible? Oh, Edward, I always thought I was rather staid and dull!'

'No, I'm afraid not,' he replied quite seriously. 'I really need someone older, someone more settled.'

'I hope that you find her,' Sara said, quite sincerely.

'So do I.' A little awkwardly, he retrieved the ring from his pocket and held it out to her. 'You don't have to give this back, you know. You're entitled to keep it.'

'No, I couldn't possibly do that,' she said at once.

Edward looked rather relieved. Then he looked down at his feet, as if he didn't know quite what to say to her.

'Er—do you want a lift back to London?' he said at last.

She shook her head. 'No, thanks. In fact, I—I might not be leaving,' she admitted, startling herself with her own words.

Surprise crossed Edward's face. 'You've met someone? Here?'

'In a way. Actually, I already knew him. It's someone I met in South America.'

He nodded slowly, as if he suddenly understood. 'You were never quite the same after you came back, Sara.'

'No, I wasn't,' she agreed softly.

There was another rather awkward silence, which was finally broken by Edward.

'I'm sorry that things haven't worked out between us. I really think this is for the best, though. I'm very fond of you, but I don't think that you'd have been the ideal marriage partner for me.'

'I think you're right,' Sara agreed, slightly amazed that the break between them had been so painless.

Edward seemed to have run out of words. He gave a rather embarrassed cough. Then he glanced at his watch. 'Well, it's nearly time for breakfast. I suppose I'd better get back to the house. I hope things work out well for you in the future, Sara.'

He walked off fairly quickly, leaving Sara with the impression that he was very relieved the engagement had been broken off in such a civilised fashion. And he was probably equally relieved that she had remained so calm. There was nothing Edward hated more than an emotional scene.

Now that part of her life had been put behind her, though, there were other—and much harder—decisions to be made. And yet, they weren't nearly as difficult as she had expected them to be. They just took a little courage—and she was finding that she had more of that than she had ever thought.

Instead of following Edward back to the house, Sara began to walk away from it. The grounds lay in front of her, green and tranquil in the early-morning sunshine, and she enjoyed the sense of peace that she found out here.

A small side-path wandered off through the trees and, without hesitation, she followed it. Then a hand slid around her waist as someone fell into step beside her.

'I like this time of the morning,' remarked Lucas. 'Apart from anything else, it gives me the opportunity to get you to myself.'

Sara's legs immediately went weak. It was something that kept happening whenever Lucas was around but, for some reason, it didn't bother her any more.

'There's something I suppose I ought to tell you,' she said a few moments later. 'I've just given Edward back his ring.'

'Of course you have,' agreed Lucas comfortably, not sounding in the least surprised. 'You should have done it a long time ago, and saved us all a lot of hassle.'

'Just because I've broken off my engagement to Edward, that doesn't mean——' she began indignantly. Then she gave a resigned sigh. Of course it meant something. Quite a lot, in fact. It meant that she didn't love Edward, but she most certainly loved Lucas Farraday. It felt marvellous to be able to admit it—frightening, but *marvellous*. Like a great blaze of light inside her head and her body.

Lucas was looking at her face rather intently, and she had the feeling that he was very easily reading the emotions clearly written there.

'Sorted it all out in your mind at last, Sara?' he said softly.

'I suppose so,' she admitted. Then she glared at him with mock severity. 'Did you know all along that you were going to win in the end?'

'There were times when it seemed pretty touch and go. And letting you come back to England on your own was a gamble. I was sure that you were attracted to me,' Lucas said ruefully. 'It was just getting you to *admit* it that was so damned hard. You were so scared of loving someone.'

'I'm still scared,' she confessed.

'Of course you are, sweetheart. It's a scary thing, tying your life up with someone else's. But between the two of us we'll make the whole thing a roaring success.'

The house was lost from sight now, as the path wandered on through a small copse of trees. Birds trilled happily overhead, the sun was getting warmer by the minute, and butterflies were beginning to flutter around the wild flowers that were pushing their way through the rather overgrown grass.

Lucas came to a halt a few yards further on. 'I think this is far enough.'

'Far enough for what?'

'To kiss you, without everyone from the house lining up to watch.' When Sara didn't raise a single protest, he lifted one dark blond eyebrow. 'Are you going to give in without a fight this time?'

'It rather looks like it,' she agreed, blissfully surrendering to something that had probably been inevitable since the first day she had seen Lucas Farraday.

'In that case, I'd better take advantage of all this co-operation before you change your mind.'

His kiss was warm and very thorough. When it was finally over, Sara gave a small sigh of pleasure.

'Can we do that just once more, before we go back for breakfast?' she asked.

Lucas grinned. 'Who said anything about going back for breakfast?'

She instantly became slightly flustered. 'But—your guests—they'll be waiting for you.'

'They're Mike's guests, not mine,' he pointed out. 'Anyway, by the time we get back to the house, they should all be gone.'

'Gone?' squeaked Sara. 'Gone where?'

'I'm sending them home,' Lucas informed her calmly.

'But—you can't! They've come for the weekend. Your mother's doing all the catering——'

'Oh, yes, my mother,' he said reflectively. 'She told me she'd met you. Did you like her?'

'She's very charming.'

'And my sisters?'

'They're very nice, too.'

'Good,' he said, with some satisfaction. 'Unfortunately, you won't be seeing them for a while. I've sent them home as well.' He glanced at his watch. 'I reckon it should take about an hour to give everyone breakfast, and then clear them out of the house,' he said thoughtfully. 'What do you think we should do until then, to pass the time?'

'I think you should go straight back and tell everyone that they can stay,' Sara said, her voice still shocked. 'What about your friend, Mike? He's the one who arranged this weekend. What's he going to say when he finds you've kicked out all these people he's invited?'

'He already knows. And he's very sympathetic,' Lucas said cheerfully. 'He's crazy about a girl called Rosie, so he understands that there are times when you have to put true love before anything else—even friendship!' With a quick, neat jerk on her wrist, he pulled her down on to the grass. Then he settled himself down beside her. 'Remember Machu Picchu?' he murmured, his voice taking on a much more husky note as his mouth gently nibbled the side of her throat. 'I like making love to you in the sunshine. And we *do* have an hour to kill.'

'Then perhaps we ought to—ought to talk,' Sara got out in a rather jerky voice.

'We are talking,' he said softly, his fingers dealing deftly with the buttons on her blouse. 'It's not always necessary to use words, Sara.'

She swallowed hard, and then closed her eyes. Only that was a mistake, because he instantly took advantage of her momentary lack of attention. His fingers reached for the soft swell of her breast, and he wouldn't release her when her eyes shot wide open again.

'Remember how it felt?' he challenged her, his blue gaze suddenly blazing down into hers, no longer lazy or sleepy.

Yes, she *did*. A pulse fluttered in her throat, and she found it surprisingly hard to breathe.

'Your skin's warm—and soft—and sweet,' he murmured, as he explored further and further.

A small sound gurgled its way out of Sara's tightened throat. It was quite incomprehensible, but Lucas seemed to understand it.

'I know, sweetheart,' he said soothingly. His mouth nuzzled her breasts, which were somehow bare. Where was her blouse? Her bra? She had no idea. She didn't even remember him removing them.

The sun shone in her eyes as she lay back on the grass, and everything suddenly seemed so very familiar. The sound of Lucas's voice, the touch of his hands, and the hard pressure of his body...

There *was* something different, though. Last time, it had been far more urgent. This morning, his lovemaking was slower, almost languid, as if he felt much more sure of her, and knew that there was no need to rush.

His mouth brushed against her skin in a gentle series of caresses that made her almost want to purr with delight. Then he slid off her skirt, and lingered over the long line of her legs. She quivered as he spent long, timeless minutes exploring the satiny inner warmth of her thighs. Then she closed her eyes, almost sleepily, as his tongue licked with even sweeter intimacy. Her body seemed to be floating along on gentle waves of pleasure, and she found, to her astonishment, that she didn't care how deeply he delved, or how intensely intimate his caresses became.

He slid over her, and his movements were still leisurely. His own shirt was removed now and she slid her hands over his smooth, tanned skin with a pleasurable sense of abandonment. It was so nice to touch him without feeling *guilty*. And he did like being touched. She could tell that from the added brightness in his eyes and the slow flush of colour spreading across his cheekbones.

'For a shy girl, you're becoming very bold,' he growled with mock severity.

'I thought that it was probably all right, since I love you,' she said a little dreamily.

Lucas became very still. 'Sometimes, I wondered if I'd ever hear you say that,' he said, his voice not altogether steady. 'There were times when I just didn't know if I was going to be lucky enough to win you.'

'I thought you were sure of everything,' she teased lightly.

He looked faintly surprised. 'Is that the way I seem to you?' Then his mouth relaxed into a grin. 'I suppose I *am* sure of most things—except for you, you black-haired witch! I did everything I could to make you fall in love with me—but I wasn't really convinced I'd succeeded until I saw you hand that ring back to Edward.'

'You *saw* me?' She gave him a small dig in the ribs. 'You were spying on me?'

'Of course,' he said, without any trace of compunction. 'Don't you realise that I've just spent one of the worst nights I've ever had, wondering if you were finally going to realise you were in love with me, instead of the oh, so eligible Edward? I've been following you around like a lovesick idiot from the moment you got up—pathetic, isn't it?' he said with a grimace. 'And not at all good for my macho image,' he added darkly.

'Then perhaps we ought to do something to restore it,' Sara suggested with a demure smile.

Lucas didn't need a second invitation. His mouth hungrily returned to hers, and this time his kisses weren't so lazy. And his hands began to move much more purposefully.

Sara found that she adored the touch and the taste of him. In fact, there really wasn't anything about this man she didn't like. Of course, he did have a tendency to be a little high-handed, but she decided she could live with that. And she was finally ready to admit that she really was quite helplessly in love with him.

And that love was returned threefold. He showed it in the care he took as he removed the last of her clothes, in the gentleness of his hands, even though he was finding it harder and harder now to keep within the bounds of self-control. And perhaps more than anything she could see it in the depths of his dark blue gaze as he stared down at her, his eyes fixed on her, as if to reassure himself that she really was here with him.

The sun blazed down more warmly, glazing their skin lightly with sweat as they moved easily together.

'Did I tell you that I adore every inch of you?' Lucas murmured, his head bending to her breast. 'And I *want* you, Sara. Hell, I've never wanted anyone like this in my entire life!'

Her arms slid round him, silently telling him that he didn't have to wait any longer. He turned to her with groaning eagerness, the length of their bodies locked together from head to foot.

The hardness of his body was deliciously familiar, the rhythm they created a growing tempo which became quite unstoppable. She could feel the force of it swelling in him, and the heat flared brightly in her own body, a hot, pounding response which took her to the very edge of an unbearable pleasure and then held her there for a few breathless, mind-bending moments.

Lucas lifted his head. 'I love you,' he said in a hoarse voice, somehow finding the strength to get the words out. 'From the moment I first saw you—I love you.'

His words were all that was needed to tip her into a great chasm of endless pleasure. She took him spinning along with her, their bodies sweat-soaked and shuddering, limbs locked against limbs, their mouths joined together in a kiss that outlasted the physical delight they had found together, continuing even as they drifted slowly back to golden, sun-soaked reality.

At last, and with great reluctance, he released her lips.

'This is one hell of a way to propose,' he said thickly.

Sara looked up at him languidly. 'Is that what this is?' she murmured. 'A proposal?'

'There wasn't a lot of opportunity to get out the actual words,' he admitted, with a tired smile. 'But it was most definitely an invitation to marry me.'

She stretched contentedly. 'I'm almost tempted to say no——' Then, as she saw the shadowed look that crossed his face, she added quickly, 'That way, you'd have to propose to me all over again.'

The dark look disappeared, and Lucas gave a faint groan. 'I'm not sure that I'm capable—at least, not for a few minutes!'

Sara grinned at him. 'Only a few minutes?' she teased. 'Is this the same man who, just a short while ago, was worried about his macho image?'

'Right now, my image feels fine,' he said with a wicked smile. Then his eyes became more serious again. 'But you haven't answered my question.'

'Yes,' she said simply.

'You'll give up that house of yours that you were so determined to hang on to, and come here to live with me?'

'Yes.'

'You'll promise that you'll stay with me for the rest of our lives?'

'Yes.'

Lucas relaxed. 'I wonder what else I should ask you, while you're in such an amenable mood?' he murmured.

'You could ask me if grass brings me out in a rash,' she said practically.

'What?' He jumped to his feet, and pulled her up beside him. Then he turned her round, and examined the faint mottling that patterned her skin. 'Oh, hell,' he said helplessly. 'Why didn't you tell me?'

'Because I didn't want you to stop,' she replied simply.

'Did the same thing happen in South America?'

'No, it didn't. Different sort of grass, I suppose.' She pulled a regretful face. 'I suppose it means we won't be able to do this again—unless we go back to Peru!'

'Of course we will,' Lucas said cheerfully. 'But next time, we'll bring a blanket! And don't worry. You still look beautiful, even when you're covered in blotches.'

'Love really *is* blind,' she remarked, with a grin. Then she leant against him with a contented sigh. 'What are we going to do for the rest of today?' she murmured.

'If you stand so close to me in all that gorgeous nakedness, I can tell you exactly what *I'll* have to do,' Lucas said huskily. 'Which will rather mess up the plans that I've already made.'

'What plans?'

'For a start, my mother's invited us to dinner.' He gave a wry smile. 'The invitation was rather premature when she made it. She just assumed that we'd manage to sort things out between us, though. She wants the dinner to be your formal introduction to my family—not that I suppose there'll be anything very formal about it! My sisters will make sure of that.'

'What about your father?' she asked. 'You haven't mentioned him.'

'He died just after Josie was born,' replied Lucas. 'After that, I was the only male in a houseful of females. Perhaps that's why I'm so good with women,' he added, lightly nibbling her ear. 'I've had a lot of practice at living with them.'

'You're living with just *one* female from now on,' Sara informed him sternly. And she was pleased to see that Lucas seemed perfectly happy with that arrangement.

'Right now, though,' went on Lucas, 'I think that we ought to get dressed again.'

'You're very prudish all of a sudden,' she mocked him lightly. 'I thought that *I* was the one who was meant to be rather strait-laced.'

'Sweetheart, I'm quite happy to walk around naked for the rest of the day,' Lucas grinned at her. 'Particularly when you're in the same state. But I can see Mike walking through the trees towards us. He's probably come to tell us that everyone has left, and we've got the house to ourselves.'

'Oh!' squeaked Sara. A little frantically, she began to wriggle into her clothes. 'How near is he?' she muttered, struggling with buttons.

'I'd say you'd got about another twenty seconds to make yourself decent,' he predicted. He had already slid into jeans and sweatshirt, and was looking far more respectable than he had any right to. 'And you'd better wipe that smile off your face and stop looking so starry-eyed, or Mike's going to know exactly what we've been up to,' he added, his blue gaze glinting very brightly.

Sara hurriedly stopped smiling, but she didn't think she could do anything about the stars in her eyes. She had the feeling that they had been there ever since Lucas had first kissed her.

And it looked as if they were going to stay there for the rest of her life.

Harlequin Presents·

Coming Next Month

#1295 ONE MORE NIGHT Lindsay Armstrong
Evonne expected to be helping a young untried writer to organize and finish his book. It was a favor to her employer. Instead, Rick Emerson was a sophisticated, attractive, dangerous specimen who constantly disturbed her

#1296 MY DESTINY Rosemary Hammond
When detective Stephen Ryan made it clear he wanted to see more of her, Joanna remembered the last man she'd loved. Three years ago she'd been married to Ross, also a policeman, and he'd died in the line of duty. Couldn't the same thing happen to Stephen?

#1297 FREE SPIRIT Penny Jordan
Hannah Maitland knew exactly what she wanted out of life, and men didn't rate very high on her list. She'd never been tempted away from her chosen path until she went to work for Silas Jeffreys.

#1298 A MOST UNSUITABLE WIFE Roberta Leigh
Her modeling career hadn't prepared her for child caring—but Lorraine was determined to care for her brother's children, orphaned by an accident. It wasn't easy—and her arrogant, authoritarian neighbor Jason Fletcher only added to her problems...

#1299 LOVE IS FOR THE LUCKY Susanne McCarthy
Ros had learned her lesson about men long ago and now kept her emotions firmly controlled. Then Jordan Griffin came on the scene tempting her to weaken—though she couldn't see why a famous rock star would be interested in her

#1300 RENDEZVOUS IN RIO Elizabeth Oldfield
Christa had been forced to leave Jefferson Barssi because of his arrogance and hard-heartedness. She and their son had been away from Brazil for six months. Now she was forced to return—and Jefferson didn't seem to have changed at all!

#1301 STEEL TIGER Kay Thorpe
Jan thought that Don Felipe de Rimados wanted a secretary. Actually he wanted a son! She was attracted to him, but could she possibly comply with her unusual contract of employment—only to walk away afterward?

#1302 THREAT OF POSSESSION Sara Wood
Roxy Page was stunned when she inherited Carnock—after all, she was only the housekeeper's daughter. Ethan Tremaine would go to any lengths to have the house back in the family, so she knew she'd have to be on guard against him.

Available in September wherever paperback books are sold, or through Harlequin Reader Service:

In the U.S.
901 Fuhrmann Blvd.
P.O. Box 1397
Buffalo, N.Y. 14240-1397

In Canada
P.O. Box 603
Fort Erie, Ontario
L2A 5X3

From America's favorite author
coming in September

JANET DAILEY

For Bitter Or Worse

Out of print since 1979!

Reaching Cord seemed impossible. Bitter, still confined to a wheelchair a year after the crash, he lashed out at everyone. Especially his wife.

"It would have been better if I hadn't been pulled from the plane wreck," he told her, and nothing Stacey did seemed to help.

Then Paula Hanson, a confident physiotherapist, arrived. She taunted Cord into helping himself, restoring his interest in living. Could she also make him and Stacey rediscover their early love?

Don't miss this collector's edition—last in a special three-book collection from Janet Dailey.

Harlequin Superromance®

THE LIVING WEST

Where men and women must be strong in both body and spirit; where the lessons of the past must be fully absorbed before the present can be understood; where the dramas of everyday lives are played out against a panoramic setting of sun, red earth, mountain and endless sky....

Harlequin Superromance is proud to present this powerful new trilogy by Suzanne Ellison, a veteran Superromance writer who has long possessed a passion for the West. Meet Joe Henderson, whose past haunts him—and his romance with Mandy Larkin; Tess Hamilton, who isn't sure she can make a life with modern-day pioneer Brady Trent, though she loves him desperately; and Clay Gann, who thinks the cultured Roberta Wheeler isn't quite woman enough to make it in the rugged West....

Please join us for HEART OF THE WEST (September 1990), SOUL OF THE WEST (October 1990) and SPIRIT OF THE WEST (November 1990) and see the West come alive!